The Nanny's Family Wish

HELEN LACEY

HARLEQUIN
SPECIAL
EDITION

HARLEQUIN®
SPECIAL EDITION™

Recycling programs for this product may not exist in your area.

ISBN-13: 978-1-335-89457-1

The Nanny's Family Wish

Copyright © 2020 by Helen Lacey

This edition published by arrangement with Harlequin Books S.A.

For questions and comments about the quality of this book, please contact us at CustomerService@Harlequin.com.

Harlequin Enterprises ULC
22 Adelaide St. West, 40th Floor
Toronto, Ontario M5H 4E3, Canada
www.Harlequin.com

Printed in U.S.A.

Helen Lacey grew up reading *Black Beauty* and *Little House on the Prairie*. These childhood classics inspired her to write her first book when she was seven, a story about a girl and her horse. She loves writing for Harlequin Special Edition, where she can create strong heroes with soft hearts and heroines with gumption who get their happily-ever-afters. For more about Helen, visit her website, helenlacey.com.

Books by Helen Lacey

Harlequin Special Edition

The Culhanes of Cedar River

The Soldier's Secret Son
When You Least Expect It

The Cedar River Cowboys

Three Reasons to Wed
Lucy & the Lieutenant
The Cowgirl's Forever Family
Married to the Mom-to-Be
The Rancher's Unexpected Family
A Kiss, a Dance & a Diamond
The Secret Son's Homecoming

The Fortunes of Texas: The Lost Fortunes

Her Secret Texas Valentine

The Fortunes of Texas

A Fortunes of Texas Christmas

The Prestons of Crystal Point

The CEO's Baby Surprise

Visit the Author Profile page at Harlequin.com for more titles.

For Robert—now and forever

Chapter One

Annie Jamison took a deep breath, clutching the resignation letter between her fingers. Quitting was never easy. And she knew her boss wouldn't take it well. There would be questions. Demands. And annoyance and irritation, too.

Actually, it probably wouldn't even register, since irritation was classed as an *emotion* and David McCall was a robot.

Of course, he wasn't really a robot. He was a flesh-and-blood man.

She'd worked as his nanny for over four years. And in truth, Annie loved the work. She especially loved his kids. Jasper and Scarlett were wonderful children and being their nanny was a joy.

But…

I can't do it forever.

Because Annie wanted her own life and not one that revolved around David and his adorable children. She was thirty-three years old and hadn't had a boyfriend since forever. And that wasn't going to change if she spent every waking hour thinking about David McCall's needs, and not her own.

No, her resignation was a long time coming. Sure, David was generous—she had the privacy of her own suite in one part of the house, drove a top-of-the-range Jeep supplied by her employer and received a Christmas bonus every year. But none of that mattered. At some point, Annie knew she had to start considering herself.

She'd been planning this move quietly for weeks. For months. Heck, for the last year. It was a secret she'd been holding close to her chest, only sharing her intent with stepsister Tess, who had remarried her ex, rancher Mitch Culhane ten months earlier and now had a baby of her own. Mitch was David's cousin and best friend, and although David didn't have the Culhane surname, he was certainly one of them in character.

The Culhanes were one of the oldest families in the county. On the Triple C, Mitch ran cattle and also bred and trained some of the best quarter horses in the state. By comparison, the McCall ranch was smaller, more of a hobby farm, but it was a beautiful place to live and raise children.

Except they're not my children. They belong to another woman.

David's wife, Jayne, and his mother, Sandra, had both been killed in an airplane crash over four and a half years earlier. The family had closed ranks after the accident. All six Culhane siblings had tried their best to shelter David and his children, even as they struggled with their own problems. They were close, good friends as well as family. And for the last few years, Annie had been welcomed into the fold and made to feel like one of them.

Which was about to change. She needed to forge her own life, away from David, his kids and Cedar River. With a population of over three thousand, the small town sat quietly in the shadow of the Black Hills of South Dakota. Once a vibrant mining town, now it was used as a stopover for people going through to the state line. There were several dude ranches in the area, as well as thriving cattle and horse ranches, and plenty of activities to keep the tourists entertained. And of course, the renowned O'Sullivan hotel. She loved Cedar River, but knew she needed to move on. If she stayed in town, Annie knew she was bound to run into David and the kids all the time—and that would simply be too hard to bear.

Annie headed down the hallway and stopped outside David's office. It was a Saturday – usually his day off, but she knew his grandmother was watching the kids for an hour while he worked. He owned a large accounting and financial planning practice in town and had clients from across the county. He was well respected in his field and very successful. He was also a good and caring dad, and she knew he loved his kids.

She sighed, squared her shoulders and knocked on the door.

"Yeah…come in."

Annie opened the door and stood on the threshold. The office had timber flooring, a couple of filing cabinets against one wall, a large white board against another, two computers and a stack of files on a desk in the center of the room.

Annie stared at him and a familiar feeling wound through her system. He was staring at the computer screen, tapping on keys, his dark-framed glasses perched on the edge of his nose. His brown hair flopped over his forehead, and the dark denim shirt he wore stretched over his broad shoulders. During the week, he preferred formal pants, shirt and tie— but on the weekend he dressed casually. She always thought it was a good look on him. Too good.

"Can I talk to you?"

He waved a hand to usher her into the room, not glancing up. "Sure."

She stepped into the room and closed the door. It was a conversation that required privacy. She certainly didn't want the kids to overhear. Because, she knew without a doubt, that David wouldn't accept her resignation easily.

"Um…"

The words sat on the edge of her tongue, tormenting her. He was still looking down. Still immersed in his work. Completely oblivious even though they were in the same room.

She tried again. "David? Hello? I can come back if you're really busy, but it's kind of important…" Her voice trailed off when she realized that his focus was so complete that he hadn't heard a word.

His disengagement fueled her frustration and her determination to do what she planned. He really had all the sensitivity of a rock.

"David!"

The sharpness in her tone quickly got his attention and he paused, midtype. "What is it?"

Annie sucked in a breath. "I'm leaving."

He glanced at her. "Sure, see you later," he said and then averted his attention back to the computer screen.

"No."

He sighed impatiently and looked at her. "What?"

Annie pushed strength into her knees and walked toward him, dropping the envelope on his desk, before steeping back a little. "I'm leaving," she said again.

He looked at her, then the envelope, then back to her. "I don't understand. What's this?" he asked and motioned to the white envelope.

"My letter of resignation," she said quietly, waiting for the pin to drop in the room.

When one didn't, she crossed her arms and waited for him to respond.

"Ah…what did you say?"

"My resignation," she said again. "Like I said, I'm leaving."

He tilted the chair back, pushed his glasses up a little and stared at her, his handsome face etched with a frown. "What's this about, Annie?"

"I'm giving you two weeks' notice," she replied and drew in a shallow breath. "That should be enough time to find a replacement."

"A replacement?" His words echoed around the room as he lifted the envelope. "You can't be serious?"

"Perfectly," she replied, trying to breathe.

"What's going on?" he asked.

She tried to shrug, tried to look confident, tried to do anything other than stand like a statue. But her feet were stuck to the floor. She noticed the tiny furrow between his brows, and the expression he made when he wasn't pleased. And then she thought about how ridiculous it was that she knew his moods and expressions so well. It was foolhardy to think about how much she knew about David. He was her boss. End of story.

"It's time I moved on from here," she said and shrugged. "No job lasts forever."

He didn't break their gaze and sat back in the chair, tapping his fingers on the desk. "I see. So my children are merely a *job* to you?"

His words were exactly what she expected. "I hate to point out the obvious, David...but taking care of them *is* a job that you pay me to do."

His stare narrowed. "Is that what this is about? Do you want a raise?"

Irritation wound up her spine. "Of course not. You're already very generous."

"Not generous enough, obviously," he said and got to his feet. "Okay, how's a ten-percent increase sound? And an extra week attached to your annual vacation time?"

Of course, it was all about the numbers. He was so blind he hadn't even bothered to ask if it was personal. Because David didn't see her as anything other than a member of his staff, someone on the payroll, as much an employee as a ranch hand.

"I don't want any more money," she said firmly. "I want to leave."

His frown deepened as he moved around the desk. "This is a little unexpected, Annie. I thought you were happy here."

At last, she thought, some level of sensitivity from the man. "I have been. However, things change and—"

"Have you been headhunted?" he asked bluntly. "I know there are several families around here who would like to hire you."

She shook her head. "No. This is...personal."

"Personal?" he echoed, still frowning. "What does that mean?"

"It means," she said with emphasis, "that it's *personal*. And I'd prefer to leave it at that."

"I'm sure you would," he said quietly. "But I after all these years, I think I deserve a little more of an explanation."

Of course, she thought irritably. It was about what *he* wanted. What *he* demanded.

Annie glared at him, aware that they were suddenly only a couple of feet apart and she had to tilt her head to look up and meet his penetrating gaze. If he wanted the whole story, he'd get it. She pushed back her shoulders, glaring hotly into his eyes, and spoke.

"All right," she said on a huff. "The truth is… I want to get married."

David Culhane McCall was rarely at a loss for words. But Annie's stunt shocked the hell out of him.

Maybe he should have seen it coming. Maybe the way she'd been quieter than usual lately, almost distracted, should have gotten him thinking that something was brewing. But…it was *Annie*. Reliable. Steadfast. A rock. The best thing that had happened to him in the last four years.

Well, not to *him*, he corrected himself immediately. But to his family. And specifically, to his kids. They adored her, and rightly so. She was an angel sent to help when life was at its worst. He'd lost his wife *and* his mother…the whole family was grieving and dealing with the profound loss and his children hadn't taken to any of the other nannies he'd employed. But Annie Jamison was different. Younger, certainly, and with less experience than the prison warden who'd come before her, and who had lasted only a week before he'd told her to leave. Annie was like a breath of fresh air compared to that. Funny and creative and smart, someone who lit up any room she entered. Someone who he relied upon to help raise his children.

Maybe you rely on her too much.

Ignoring the voice in his head, he looked into her upturned face. Her blue eyes shone brilliantly; her full mouth was set in an unusually tight line instead of her usual glowing smile and her cheeks were flushed. She looked…angry. A few strands of honey-brown hair had escaped from the ponytail she always wore and were tucked behind her ears. She was incredibly pretty. Not in an overt or flashy way, but a quiet kind of beauty—not that he ever thought about Annie in that way. That was inappropriate. Out of the question. She was the nanny. His employee. His friend, he had believed.

Except she wasn't looking at him in a friendly way. In fact, she looked madder than hell. Married? She'd said she wanted to get *married*? He ignored he way his gut tightened at the idea.

"Married?" he echoed the word incredulously. As far as he knew, she wasn't dating anyone. "Who the hell to?"

She shrugged. "I don't know. I guess I jumped

the gun there a bit. But I want the chance to meet someone I can care about, maybe enough to marry and spend the rest of my life with. And I can't do that while I'm…while I'm…"

"While you're what?" he demanded, so confused his head spun. He didn't really understand what she was saying. She wanted to get married, but not to anyone in particular? It didn't make sense.

"Living here," she replied and sighed. "Living this life. With your children as…" She stopped, swallowing hard. "Almost as if they are…" Her words trailed again. "I want my own family, my own children. And to do that, I need to leave."

David stared at her and sucked in a breath. She wanted children? But not his? How could anyone not want his kids – they were incredible.

He inhaled again and her perfume swirled through the air. Or maybe it was her shampoo. He wasn't sure, but the scent was as familiar to him as any on the ranch—vanilla and spice—a sweet combination that always pleased his senses. He wasn't sure why. But it had become her signature scent over the years, a way of knowing she was close, part of things, keeping the balance, making things easier.

"So, you're not leaving us *to get* married?" he asked and scowled.

"I will eventually. Who knows," she said and flapped her arms. "It's really not anyone's business. Look, you asked the question, and I answered it." She pointed to the envelope. "There's my resignation. I'll be going in two weeks, that should give you enough time to advertise for my replacement and conduct interviews."

David rocked back onto his heels. "No."

Her bottom lip dropped. "No?"

He crossed his arms. "I don't accept your resignation," he said and then moved around the desk, shaking his head in confusion. "I just don't get it, Annie. You've always seemed happy here. Happy with us."

Her expression remained tight. "I love the kids. I always will. But accept it, or not, David…it won't change the fact that I'm leaving."

He stared at her, trying to read something in her expression that would indicate she wasn't as determined as her words made it seem. But all he saw was steely resolve and a budding antagonism.

And his children, he knew, wouldn't understand. They would feel her loss. They'd grieve it, would be heartbroken. Four-and-half-year-old Scarlett adored her, and eight-year-old Jasper hung on her every word. They would be devastated by the news. Inconsolable. The very notion made him ache through to his bones.

"You can't leave us," he said simply.

Something flickered across her face, shadowed her eyes for a moment. But then the resolve was back. "I have to, David."

He let out a heavy breath. "Annie, please don't do this."

She didn't flinch. "I'm sorry," she said as she

left the room, leaving the scent of her shampoo in her wake.

David wasn't sure how long he remained in the office, staring after the opened doorway. Minutes. Hours. No, he corrected, not hours. Only, time had suddenly stretched into some weird vortex and he couldn't think straight. Of all the things he might expect, Annie's leaving was not on the list. She was practically a part of their family, and he'd always appreciated everything she did for his children.

So, how on earth was he supposed to tell them that she was leaving? Dread formed in his stomach as he headed from the room and down the hall, making his way toward the kitchen at the rear of the house.

His grandmother Mittie McCall was standing behind the counter, her wild red hair piled high on her head, her long, handcrafted wooden earrings dangling from her ears. Mittie always made him smile. She was his father's mother, an adventurous and free-spirited woman who had made the ranch her home, but spent a good part of each year travelling the globe. When David was two years old, his father, James McCall died unexpectedly from a heart attack while out mustering cattle. David's mother, Sandra, remarried Ivan Petrovic when he was six and then had Leah, his half sister. David had always considered Ivan to be his dad, as the older man had always treated him like his son, but he kept his real father's name out of respect for Mittie and the generations of

McCalls before him. Family was important. Family mattered above everything else.

And his had just imploded!

Annie...

He got back to thinking about her. And his shock at her announcement.

"'Morning, sweetpea."

David grimaced at the nickname his grandmother had been calling him for decades. "Hey, Nan."

She smiled. "I've made cookies."

Mittie was a perennial baker. "The kids will be happy. Speaking of my kids, where are they?"

"In the stables with Annie," she replied and smiled again, waving a spatula covered in chocolate frosting. "Something about a cat having kittens."

David nodded, then walked from the kitchen and through the mud room, grabbing his coat from the peg by the door. It was cool outside, the sky rumbling and cloudy and rain looked imminent. October was traditionally cool and this one was proving to be harsher than usual, David thought as he shouldered into his coat and hiked up the collar. The stables were around the front, so he circumnavigated the house and within minutes the dogs Rufus and Daisy were racing around his feet, trying to get him to play chase with a stick. The fluffy pair weren't exactly ranch hounds...more like lap dogs. But the kids loved them and that was all that mattered.

He'd bought them as pups not long after Jayne and his mom had been killed, as a way to help his children with their loss and overcome the incredible pain they were feeling. It wasn't nearly enough, of course. But six months later, he'd made the solid decision to hire Annie, and things got better. Time was a healer, too. So was work. And family. Despite everything that had happened, David was grateful for all he had in his life. And up until half an hour ago, he'd been incredibly grateful for Annie. Now he was just annoyed.

He stalled in the doorway, watching the trio. His children and the woman they adored. Annie had been a pivotal part of their lives for so long it would be difficult to imagine life on the ranch without her. Almost impossible. She created balance and harmony. She was the steadiness they all needed after so much loss and was an essential part of their everyday lives. She was…family.

He watched as Scarlett clutched her hand as they bent over, looking into a small box in the corner of the stables. Jasper said something and Annie laughed, the sound echoing and somehow hitting him directly in the center of the chest. It occurred to him that he hadn't heard her laugh much lately. Oh, sure, sometimes when she was in the garden with Mittie or in the kitchen with the kids, or reading the paper with his dad when his father dropped in. But around him…not so much.

Had it always been like that? Had he simply been blinded by the fact she was essential to his kids and therefore didn't think about *their* relationship. Not that they actually *had* a relationship. She worked for him. She lived in his house. They ate dinner together with the kids most weeknights. They talked about the children, the weather and other mundane things, but never about anything really personal. Of course, he'd done a background check before hiring and knew all about her. He knew her stepsister, as well as her father and stepmother. She loved chocolate and hated avocado and always ordered her pizza with extra mushrooms. She was an early riser, but was often asleep on the sofa by nine in the evening. The woman jogged three mornings a week and some Sundays and did yoga downtown on Thursday evenings. He knew she liked reading murder mysteries. She loved Christmas and holidays and spent forever searching for the right gifts. Annie had a sweet voice and would often sing the kids to sleep with a lullaby. She cried every time she watched *The Notebook*. He knew she liked to wear knitted scarves in winter. He knew she liked to dance, listened to country music and had a hankering for George Strait and Kenny Chesney love songs.

But what he didn't know was why in the hell she was leaving him.

Not *me,* he corrected, but the kids, their family, and the life she had on the ranch.

Again, he remembered she'd said something about getting married, registered that it irked him and didn't want to think about why. Besides, she hadn't mentioned she was seeing anyone. Maybe he'd been wrong…maybe she *was* dating someone. It wasn't as though he paid a lot of attention to her love life. Although, if she was in a relationship, she was certainly discreet about it to the point of keeping the guy invisible.

Yep, it definitely irked him—a lot—which he knew wasn't rational. Annie could do whatever she liked. Still, he didn't like secrets. And really, she could still have a relationship and work for him. Most people balanced a professional and personal life. He even did it himself occasionally. Although he was hard pressed to remember the last time he'd been on a date. And he hadn't had sex in forever, not since Rachel had left town over a year earlier. She'd worked at the local hospital in the surgical unit and they'd had a mutually agreeable *no-commitment-required* relationship for about eight months. The no-strings arrangement suited them both. When she left town to pursue her career in Boise, neither of them was exactly heartbroken. Sure, he'd liked Rachel, but she would never have been someone he could settle down with permanently. For one, she didn't want kids, and since he already had two of his own, imagining they could have anything long-term or serious was out of the question. Besides, he wasn't in love with her. He liked her well enough, but that was it. They hadn't even really been friends…more like two people who occasionally got together for dinner and sex. Which had suited them both.

Since then, David hadn't been inclined to try

meeting anyone. His accounting practice kept him busy and so did the kids. His children were everything to him, and frankly, he wasn't sure he wanted another live-in nanny, either. He'd actually known Annie for a long time, having met her at his cousin Mitch's first wedding to her stepsister, a decade earlier. Their paths had crossed several times in the ensuing years, mostly at the holidays or weddings and funerals.

Then when Jayne died, his whole world shifted. When Annie applied for the nanny position, employing her had been a no-brainer. She was familiar, she already knew Jasper, and Scarlett was only eight months old at the time. Having her move to the ranch was also an easy decision. But allowing someone new the same option didn't sit right. He didn't want a stranger interacting with his kids, living down the hall from them. From him.

He only wanted Annie, end of story.

"Daddy!"

Scarlett's animated voice cut through his thoughts and she came racing toward him, landing against his legs with a resounding thump. He hauled her into his arms and she hugged him tightly. David kissed her rosy cheek and smiled. Everything about his baby girl made him happy. She was a delightful child, sweet natured and fun loving, and he knew much of that was Annie's doing. Jasper was the more serious of the pair, but he had also flourished under Annie's guidance and affection. David knew, without a doubt, that Annie loved his children. He looked in her direction and their gazes clashed, registering somewhere deep down and in a way that made him catch a breath. She wasn't smiling now.

"The kittens are here, Daddy," Scarlett said excitedly. "Come and see."

"Okay, sweetie."

His daughter squirmed out of his arms, grabbed his hand and dragged him into the corner of the stable. "Look."

David peered into the small, makeshift birthing box he suspected Rudy, the ranch foreman who'd been with him for a long time, had constructed. David noticed several tiny babies moving around. The mommy cat was still in the process of birthing and he watched as his children observed the wonder of nature. One thing about living on a ranch, the reproductive process was never something to shy away from. If it wasn't the stable cat, it was one of the cows or the chickens. And he liked that they had the opportunity to witness birth and sometimes death, in a way that was open and honest and safe. It was the frame he used to comfort them when they asked about their mom, which happened less and less as the years passed. His fault, he suspected. And it wasn't that he didn't want to talk about Jayne or dilute her memory—it was just so hard to make sense of it.

And now they would lose Annie, too.

"Bubbles is going to be the best mommy ever," Jasper stated. "Don't you think, Annie?"

David noticed that she flicked a glance in his direction. "Of course."

Bubbles was, in fact, a stray who had turned up a few weeks earlier and who had decided the shelter of the stables and the supply of mice at suppertime was a good reason to hang around. The cat was friendly and affectionate, if not a little timid, and once the kittens were weaned and rehomed, David figured he'd get the cat neutered and let her stay on. Admittedly, he was more of a dog person, but the kids liked her, and that in and of itself was enough reason to make her a part of things.

"Can I keep one of the kittens, Dad?" Jasper asked and grinned, pointing to the box.

"We'll see," he replied and touched his son's head, staying close for a few moments.

"The black one with the white feet," Jasper said and chuckled as he pointed to one of the kittens. "I can call him Socks."

David smiled. Jasper's logic was an endearing quality. "Sure."

"Can we keep that one too," Jasper queried and pointed to a little black kitten that Bubbles was cleaning up. "I mean, one for me and one for Scarlett," he explained, still grinning. "And probably one for Annie, too. And Aunt Leah. Oh, and great-grandma. And Pop likes cats, so we should save one for him."

He had to admit, his son was quite the negotiator, since most of the kittens had now been accounted for.

"So, I don't get a kitten?" he asked, still smiling.

"You can have Bubbles," Jasper announced, still all logic and David figured the apple didn't fall far from the tree.

The last kitten had arrived and he reminded the kids to remain quiet while the cat went about her business. Annie was silent, watching the birth, biting her lower lip as she often did when deep in thought. He noticed how Scarlett was back holding her hand, standing close to the woman she adored, and again he was overcome with the feeling that life would be very different when Annie left the ranch.

That thought gathered momentum in his gut until it threatened to cut off air to his lungs. He wanted to understand her feelings…but damn, his kids were going to be crushed. And that was unacceptable. Plus, two weeks wasn't enough time to find a replacement…or to convince her to stay.

"Annie," he said quietly. "Can I talk to you for a minute?"

She met his gaze and hesitated for a moment before releasing Scarlett. David watched as she moved away from the birthing box and then followed until they were out of earshot from the kids.

"What?" she asked tersely.

He turned, crossing his arms, making sure the children couldn't hear him. "Two things," he said quietly. "Firstly, I'll need more time to find some-one to replace you, so I want a month's notice. Sec-ondly," he said, dropping his voice a fraction. "I'm not going to play bad cop for you, Annie. If you want to leave, you're going to have to tell the kids yourself."

She glared at him, and David knew he'd backed her into a corner. She adored his kids; he knew that. She'd never do anything to hurt them.

Except leave them, apparently.

Well, one thing was certain. He wasn't going to let her go without a damned good fight!

Chapter Two

Annie took a breath, staring at him, noticing how his green eyes glittered behind his glasses. He really did have the Clark Kent thing down to a fine art. He was highly intelligent and with little patience—or skill, frankly—for small talk. He liked jazz music, didn't dance, had never smoked and rarely drank. Annie swallowed hard, trying not to think about the fact he hadn't shaved that morning and his stubble was incredibly sexy. Because thinking David was sexy was plain old stupid.

So, snap out of it...

She shrugged. "Sure, no problem."

He didn't look convinced and his mouth twisted

a little. "Go ahead, do it. We're both here…say what you need to say."

She stepped closer. "You're being impossible."

"I'm not the one abandoning them."

It was a low blow. "You know why I—"

"So you can marry some guy you haven't even met yet?"

"Who says I haven't?" she shot back, her teeth clenched tightly.

David's brows came together. "You did," he replied. "You said you didn't know who—"

"If you must know," she said, keeping her voice low, "there is someone. But I'd rather not talk about it."

"If you've got some secret lover, Annie, rest assured you can still see him and remain here…the world is full of people juggling relationships and work."

Secret lover? Hardly. But she did have someone she thought might one day become her lover… and maybe more. Twelve months earlier she'd done something completely out of character—she'd logged on to a dating site. Four months after some brief texting sessions with a couple of definite Mr. Noes, she was matched up with Byron Eckart. He was funny and charming and exactly the tonic she needed for her stuck-in-a-rut life. He was single, over thirty, six foot five and handsome in a rugged kind of way. Plus, he was a fireman—a job that he loved. The only thing was, that job was in Texas, so they'd never *actually* met. They texted, they talked on the phone, they even Facetimed—but she hadn't summoned the courage for a meeting. He'd asked, of course. And she knew it was the next step. But something held her back.

A six-foot-five, green-eyed something...

She shook off the thought. Byron was her future—maybe. She just needed the courage to take a chance on that future.

"He's not a secret." She corrected David's interpretation and sighed. "I just don't like flaunting my personal life."

His gaze narrowed, and then he raised a curious brow as though the idea of her actually having a personal life was surprising. "Who is he? Someone local?"

"No one you know," she replied hotly, holding on to her building embarrassment. She didn't want to talk to David about her love-life. Not ever. "And I'll tell the children today. Now, if you don't mind, I'll just get back to my Saturday…it is my day off, after all."

"I never stop you having your time off," he reminded her.

Which was true. Annie *chose* to spend most of her Saturdays at the ranch. The fact was, the place felt like home. It *was* her home. And although David looked after the kids on the weekend, she still enjoyed hanging out with them.

She sighed. "I know. Sorry."

"I don't want you to be sorry, Annie," he said quietly. "I want you to *stay*."

She ignored the hint of vulnerability in his voice, figuring she was imagining it, and turned, striding back toward the kids. Rudy, came out from his small cottage behind the stables and walked through the door. He stopped to speak with David for a moment, then came toward the birthing box. She'd always liked Rudy and they chatted for a few minutes, while the kids began naming the kittens. She didn't relax though…she couldn't when she knew David was near, silently listening to her every word. Making judgments, of course. Thinking he had all the answers. Believing he knew *everything* about her.

Big jerk.

It was one of his annoying qualities.

Like the way he didn't talk much. Annie was sure she regularly spoke ten words for each one he said. Over the years she'd become accustomed to his silences, or the way he could concentrate so effortlessly and give things his complete attention. He had a charitable nature, generously giving to several local organizations, including a sizable donation to the local veterans' home every year. So, he had his flaws, but David James Culhane McCall was generally a good man.

Once Bubbles and all the kittens settled, Annie left the stables and headed back to the house and made her way to her suite. She liked to call it the West Wing. A long hallway with a lockable door that offered a little distance between the rest of the house, with a bedroom, bathroom, lounge and small kitchenette. Not that she ever locked the door, nor did she cook on the stove much. But she had a good stock of fragrant teas and a box of Oreos at hand for those times when she needed to be alone. The combined living and dining areas had a lovely view overlooking the back meadow and small orchard, and she'd placed a few pieces of her own furniture around so it felt more like her own home, rather than a few rooms in someone else's house.

She put the kettle on, popped an herbal tea bag into a mug then grabbed her cell to check for messages. There was one from her sister asking if she was free for coffee the following day, and she replied with a thumbs-up emoji. Now that Tess was remarried to Mitch and had a baby, she was busy being a wife and mom, but always made time for family. Annie adored her sister and was forever grateful their parents had fallen in love so many years ago. Annie's mother had died when she was a child, much like Tess's dad, and she knew her sister was equally grateful that their parents had made them all a family.

Annie sat by the window and sipped her tea, looking out to the meadow beyond the garden and experienced a feeling of wistful yearning for everything she longed for but didn't have. Love. Children. Sex. A home to truly call her own. Perhaps one day. Once she left the ranch and her old life behind. But it would be hard. The thought of leaving the kids tore her up inside.

Still, she knew she had to do it.

Otherwise, she'd stay forever. Or until the day David remarried and she was replaced in the children's lives. For a while, Annie had imagined his old girlfriend was a prime candidate. And truthfully, she hadn't liked Rachel. What David saw in her, besides the obvious great legs and pretty face, Annie had no idea. She remembered Jayne McCall, on the few occasions they'd met, as warm and friendly with a deep love for her family and friends. Rachel seemed like the polar opposite. Totally career driven, and never at all interested in being involved in David's family. Not that Annie believed there was anything wrong with someone pursuing the career they loved—but she'd never been one to think that a job and career were *everything*. She'd spent three years at college, then got a job in Rapid City working as an admin for a member of the city council, but the hours had been long and relentless. At twenty-six, after five years in the same role, she realized she needed to make some changes in her life.

She went back to college to study education, getting her teaching degree while she worked part-time in childcare. Three years later Jayne McCall was killed, and six months after that Annie began working for David. She hadn't planned on having a career as a nanny, but when her friend Connie O'Sullivan, whose family were David's clients, mentioned that he had been unsuccessfully trying to find a nanny since his wife's death, something tripped inside her. She applied, thinking that their complicated family connection might muddy the waters, but David didn't appear bothered by the fact her sister had recently divorced his best friend and cousin.

Annie sighed, got to her feet and headed for the bedroom. She stripped off the sheets and piled them onto the floor, grabbing the clean linens she'd placed on the dresser the day before. She made the bed, plumping out the cushions and straightening the pale mauve duvet. It was a nice room. And a comfy bed. Pity she'd never had anyone in it, she thought wryly, other than Scarlett and Jasper when they jumped on her some mornings. They never intruded though. David was a stickler for *doing the right thing*. He gave her space, and insisted the kids do the same. But there were times when she couldn't resist the kids' pleas to curl up beside her as she read them a book or told them a story.

David, of course, rarely entered her *space*. The rooms were hers—he'd made that clear to her on day one. Not that he'd ever said as much, but she knew he was a stickler about appropriate behavior. He'd fixed a faucet, repaired a sticking window and occasionally wrestled a giant arachnid from the bathroom—but that was it.

Byron, she knew, didn't *do* spiders. He could run into a burning building, but a spider left him in a panic. It made her smile. And although it probably wasn't true, the idea made him rather adorable.

He genuinely seemed to like her. He'd been engaged once, a few years ago, but it hadn't lasted, and since then he hadn't had a serious girlfriend. She should have been jumping out of her skin over the *idea* of him.

Should have...

She walked past the mirror and took a long look at herself, patting her hips, thinking about the extra pounds she'd added to her frame in the past couple of months. She'd always been curvy, especially on top. When she was in high school and college her *assets* had garnered her way more attention than she was prepared for, or wanted, since she was something of an introvert. She'd spent most of her time on campus hiding her body behind baggy sweaters and ill-fitting clothes, avoiding the attention of horny college freshmen, who all seemed to be drawn to skinny blonde sorority girls anyway. Even now, old habits died hard—she tended to dress for comfort over high fashion.

Looking down at her worn jeans, long shirt and stretched-out sweater, she sighed. She really did need a makeover. Once she left, maybe she'd spend some of her savings on a new look. Maybe a new haircut, some more stylish clothes. And a vacation. Somewhere warm and where she could relax and read and decompress. Somewhere far away from David McCall and his adorable children.

Annie sighed and quickly changed into her riding jeans, a checked shirt and sheepskin-lined jacket and cowboy boots, grabbed her Stetson and returned to the stables. Rudy was still there, watching over the kittens, but David and the kids were gone.

"I'm taking Star out for a while," she said and took a headstall and lead from the peg near the tack room door. "Just for an hour or so."

The old man nodded, mentioned something about the weather looking ominous, and said he'd get the gear while Annie headed to the pasture behind the stables. Star, her thirteen-year-old buckskin gelding, raised his head the moment he caught her whistle on the wind, and whinnied as he loped to the gate. The tall gelding had been part of her life for two years; after a successful career as a cutting horse, Mitch had saved him from the slaughterhouse. His previous owner discarded him after an injury that was fixable, but costly. Annie's connection to Mitch was unavoidable since he was David's cousin and closest friend, but since he and Tess were divorced, her step-sister was never mentioned when their paths crossed. Annie had always wanted her own horse, and after a year of riding one of David's reliable mounts, decided to make Star her own. He was a sweet-natured animal, a little lazy but trustworthy and patient. His warm muzzle touched her face and she slipped on the headstall easily, then brought him through the gate and led him into the stable. She had him brushed down and tacked up quickly and then sprang onto the saddle, heeding Rudy's warning about the gray sky and how a thunderstorm was predicted.

She took the trail she usually did, around the back meadow and toward the creek that bordered the ranch and the place next door. The ranch sat on close to two hundred acres, smaller than some places in the area, but the land was good grazing. David wasn't interested in raising cattle, so he allowed Mitch to run some of his Angus herd on the place.

About a hundred feet from the creek was an old split-log cabin. It was the original homestead, built generations ago by David's great-grandparents. Rudy kept the place neat and tidy and she'd been in the cabin many times, mostly to show Jasper and Scarlett the old photographs on the mantel and tell stories about their ancestors. About David's parents —James McCall, who'd married seventeen-year old Sandra Culhane, sister to the notorious Billie-Jack Culhane—the man who'd run out on his kids when his wife had died and left his eldest son, eighteen-year-old Mitch, to raise his five younger siblings. Not that she talked about Billie-Jack. No one did, not even the Culhanes. But he was a part of the town's folklore, with his drinking and womanizing ways. James McCall, on the other hand, had been a pillar of the community, much like his only son.

Annie sighed, dismounting and tethering Star to the hitching rail outside the cabin. The creek beckoned and she headed for it, noticing a couple of birds swooping along the water. She loved hanging by the water's edge. She'd picnicked with the kids at the creek countless times. Jasper was a competent rider and had his own pony, while Star always knew when she rode double with Scarlett, as though he was well aware there was precious cargo on board. The kids loved the creek and the cabin and Annie knew it would be one of the things she would miss about being on the ranch. Just one...but there were so many more.

Thunder rumbled overhead and she looked to the sky, noticing the dark, curdling clouds. Rain spotted her shirt and she tilted her hat downward as she turned and headed for the cabin. Star was moving about, clearly agitated as the rain increased and another clap of thunder roared. Annie flinched, reaching into her side pocket for her cell to call Rudy and say she'd be staying at the cabin until the rain cleared, and then realized she'd left it in the tack bucket back at the stables. The rain increased, followed by several large rounds of thunder and lightning. Star whinnied and she heard another horse unexpectedly respond in the distance. There were no horses loose on this part of the ranch. She looked toward the trail and spotted a rider coming toward her, astride King, his tall dappled-gray gelding.

Her heart skipped a beat.

David...

She would recognize the way he sat in the saddle anywhere. He might not be a typical cowboy, but he certainly rode like one. The rain quickly fell heavier, and Annie suspected she should head for the cabin, but watching him ride through the storm, his swagger so familiar, nothing could make her drag her gaze away. He wore a raincoat and the tail flapped as the horse jogged toward her.

He came to a halt about ten feet away, his expression as dark and thunderous as the sky above them. And then he spoke. Well, more like he yelled.

"What the hell are you doing?"

The moment David saw Annie heading off on her horse, he realized she would get stuck in the rainstorm. He knew enough about the South Dakota weather to suspect the storm would be a bad one. And he certainly didn't want Annie stuck out alone on a trail ride while a storm raged on around her. She should have known better. As should Rudy have, something he said to the older man when he'd barked out the instruction to saddle up King so he could follow her and bring her back to the stables before the storm hit. But too late.

He spotted her racing back from the creek, her hand on her hat to stop it blowing off her head. Of course, he knew she'd head for the old cabin. She made no secret of the fact that it was her favorite place on the ranch. His too, once a upon a time, but he rarely got down to the place anymore. There were too many memories, too many reminders of the woman he'd loved and lost.

"I've been riding," she yelled over the rain now pelting over them.

David dismounted, grabbed King's reins in one hand and strode toward Star, then quickly untied the horse. "Get up to the cabin," he shouted and led the horses toward the small barn at the side of the house. He tethered the horses inside two stalls and quickly raced back toward the cabin.

She was on the porch, hat off, her hair plastered to her head, her chest heaving and hands on her hips. "What are—"

"Exactly," he shot back as he took the steps and stood in front of her. "Why on earth would you go riding when you knew there was a storm coming?"

"I didn't think it would be this bad," she said quickly, her blue eyes flashing. "And I've ridden in the rain before. Star doesn't spook in bad weather."

Thunder clapped loudly and she flinched. "Remember the rule, Annie?" he reminded her.

"I left my cell back at the stables."

The rule. His only stipulation, really. *Call someone when things go wrong.* Like, if the car breaks down on the side of the road. If a date goes awry. If a headache turns into a migraine. If you get stuck in a thunderstorm. *If the airplane you're in has unexpected mechanical failure.*

The memory struck him deep down. And as always, he wondered what he would have said had he the chance to say some final words to his wife and also to his mother. *I love you. I'll miss you. I can't do this without you.*

David ran his gaze over the woman in front of him. "You're soaked through."

"I'm fine," she said as wind whipped across the porch and she shivered.

David pointed to the door. "Let's go inside until the rain clears."

He extracted the hidden key from its spot and unlocked the door. The scent of cedar hit him immediately and he opened the door wide to allow her to pass. She hesitated for a moment, then took off her boots and crossed the threshold. David did the same and shrugged out of the raincoat, then hung it on a peg near the door. The cabin was small and open-plan, with only a separate bedroom and tiny bathroom, which relied on a septic tank out the back. It was sparsely furnished, but there was still a table and chairs in the kitchen, and old brocade sofa near the fireplace in the living area and a few rugs scattered over the floor in various places.

"I'm sorry I barked at you before," he said flatly. "I was worried, that's all."

She shrugged fractionally. "I know, but I can take care of myself. And I love it here. I always feel safe in this cabin." She sighed. "I'm sorry though, for making you worry. I just needed to get away."

"From me?"

She nodded. "This place always helps me think."

David understood. The cabin held some great

memories. He'd spent time with Jayne in the cabin when they were first dating. It was part of the reason he ensured the place was kept clean and tidy. The memories were not something he wanted to fade away. The cabin meant a lot to him, and he realized it was the first time he'd been inside the place, alone, with a woman since Jayne had died. Not that he thought of Annie as a woman. Well, of *course* she was a woman. He might need glasses or contact lenses, but that didn't mean he couldn't see the obvious. She was, in fact, incredibly attractive. She had flawless skin, for starters, and her hair was the color of warm treacle, and her eyes were vivid, cornflower blue. She had curves, for sure, and since he wasn't made of stone it was impossible at times to *not* notice the way she moved or the way her hips swayed when she walked. It was just that he'd successfully programmed himself to ignore those thoughts because she worked for him, and it was inappropriate to think of her as anything other than the nanny.

And he never, ever crossed the line.

Once the door was closed, he figured he'd light a fire to warm them up. Heading to the fireplace, he pulled together the kindling, got the fire started, then turned and found Annie standing by the kitchen table, her wet clothes dripping water onto the floor.

"I think there are a few towels in the bathroom," he said, suddenly struck by the way her shirt clung to her curves, the thin cotton almost seeming translucent and clearly outlining her breasts. It kicked at something low in his gut, creating a kind of hazy awareness that somehow made him suck in a sharp breath. David quickly shook the feeling off and frowned. "And a few of Leah's clothes in the wardrobe. No point in you catching a cold."

Her hand came to her throat and she pulled the shirt collar together. "Sure."

He watched as she scurried toward the bathroom and waited until she was out of sight before he took another breath. Something didn't feel right. He usually knew exactly what he was feeling and thinking. But in the last few hours his thought processes had become uncharacteristically skewed. No doubt because he was mad with her for the way she'd disrupted his day, and potentially his children's lives—and his—with her plan to leave the ranch.

David pressed a palm to his chest, felt his heart thundering behind his ribs and took a few long and calming breaths. The rain on the metal roof was usually a sound that relaxed him. But now, he felt agitated and restless.

He grabbed his coat and headed back outside, quickly pulling on his boots before racing across the yard to the small shed. He cranked up the temperamental generator so they at least had some light. By the time he was back in the house, the rain was heavier and he quickly ditched his coat and shoes again and shut the front door. He spotted a couple of his sister Leah's pottery mugs on the draining board in the kitchen and smiled. The mugs were molded in the shape of farm animals and he had an entire set of them up at the main house. His sister often spent time in the cabin and had a small workshop and kiln out the back where she created her art. Mostly she sculpted pieces from metal, but she also dabbled in clay and ceramics. She was incredibly talented and he was immensely proud of her.

Perhaps Leah would be able to talk some sense into Annie, since they were friends. Or maybe he could prevail on Tess to set her straight. There was no one's opinion that mattered more to Annie than her sister's. Whoever it turned out to be, the situation clearly required an intervention.

Only, what if Tess couldn't get through to her? What if she really was in a serious relationship? What if? He hated those two words.

What if the plane hadn't crashed? What if he had asked his wife to skip flying that day? What if he'd taken the time to notice how unhappy Annie really was?

He knew one thing for sure. He had to figure out a way to convince Annie to stay.

And fast.

Annie pulled a couple of shirts out of the old wardrobe in the corner of the bedroom and tugged at the red T-shirt she'd slipped on, thinking she would prefer to change back into her soaking-wet shirt. At least that fit properly. Leah was slim and athletic, so her clothes weren't a great fit. But she needed to wear something while her shirt dried out. Annie grabbed her wet shirt and left the bedroom, coming face-to-face with David within seconds.

Without his glasses, he was just as handsome, but less serious looking.

"Contacts?" she queried. "You don't normally wear them on the weekend."

"I don't normally go horse riding in the rain, either. But glasses don't cut it in a storm. And I'm a whiz at putting in contacts in a hurry."

Annie took a step farther into the room, aware that the rain was still pelting on the roof. She walked toward the fireplace and carefully draped her shirt over the mesh fire screen.

"So, why did you?" she asked when she faced him again. "Come out in the storm, I mean."

"I didn't want you stuck out in it alone. Storms can be dangerous."

"I can take care of myself," she said.

"You forgot your cell phone," he pointed out.

Annie shrugged lightly. "You knew I'd come here, obviously. I'm fairly predictable when it comes to my horse-riding habits. And this place is perfectly safe."

"Leah got stuck here for three days once, remember?" he reminded her. "Two years ago. The creek flooded and she couldn't make it across until the rain stopped."

She did remember. They'd all been worried sick for days. "You're right. I should have taken my cell.

I'm sorry. I was just rushing and... I forgot. It was careless."

Always call. Always keep in touch. When she'd first arrived at the ranch he'd made it clear about his expectations and later she learned why. When Jayne McCall and Sandra Petrovic had died, there had been no communication, no calls, no opportunity to say goodbye. Now the whole family had texts and calls flying between them on a daily basis. At first, it had seemed suffocating and dependent...but she understood. They had all experienced an excruciating loss; keeping in touch was their way of staying connected to each other. Of letting each other know they were safe. That, yes, they *were* coming home.

"It's not a big deal, Annie... I only—"

"I know," she said, cutting him off. "I get it. I know why it's important. It's because of your mom and Jayne and I—"

"The kids would be devastated if anything happened to you."

The kids. Of course. "I know. But I'm fine." She forced a smile. "Just soaked through."

He didn't move, and when he spoke again, his voice was unusually raspy.

"Why are you doing it, Annie? Why are you really leaving us?"

Because I have to...

"I told you why," she said, dying a little inside.

"Because you want to marry some guy you've

never said a word about, never been seen with, never introduced to anyone…right?"

"It's not like that," she said and harrumphed. "Byron is—"

"Byron?" he repeated and laughed humorlessly. "Seriously? What is he…a poet or history professor or something?"

"If you must know, he's a fireman."

He frowned. "Really? Where's he stationed? Rapid City? Deadwood?"

"No," she replied. "El Paso. Texas."

The moment he realized what she meant, he made a disbelieving sound. "Since I know you've never been to Texas, that means you've never actually met this guy, right?"

"Well, I haven't—"

"Is this some kind of online love-affair thing you have going?"

"It's not a love-affair," she said, coloring from head to toe with embarrassment because he made the idea sound so ridiculous. "You're right, we've never met in person. But we've talked a lot on the phone and…" Her words trailed off and she shrugged. "I don't have to justify anything to anyone."

Or you…

That's what she really wanted to say.

"But you plan on leaving here, moving to Texas and marrying someone you have never actually met?"

"Of course not!"

"But you said you wanted to get married and—"

"I do," she defended. "You're twisting this all around. Yes, I haven't met Byron face-to-face...yet. But I...might. And if it works out...great. If not, then hopefully I'll meet someone else."

She felt better for saying it. Stronger. Like she was in complete control of her own life and her future. Even though inside, she was a quivering wreck. For one, there was something strange about the situation. Because they were alone together. Truly alone. There were no kids in the next room, no Mittie in the kitchen, no Ivan reading one of his old books in the front living room. Just the two of them. There was nowhere to escape, nowhere to avoid his luminous green eyes.

"This doesn't sound like you," he remarked.

She harrumphed. "Maybe you don't know me as well as you think you do?"

"I know you're not reckless and impulsive," he said quietly. "If you were, I would never have entrusted you with my kids."

She knew that. David cherished his children, and their well-being was paramount. "I've always appreciated your trust in me."

"Have you?" he queried and raised a brow. "You know, since my children adore you, I believe I have the right to know why you're acting as though they don't matter in all this."

"Of course they matter," she retorted. "You know how much they mean to me. But I have to do this."

"Why?"

She sucked in a breath. "Because…if I don't leave now I might—"

"Is it him?" David demanded. "Is *he* telling you to do this…this fireman boyfriend of yours?"

Annie shook her head. "It's me," she replied. "This is what *I* want."

"I don't quite believe you, Annie," he said, tilting his head a fraction and meeting her eyes with his own. "There's something else…something that you're not saying. I know you. And yes, I know you care deeply about Scarlett and Jasper. I also think you wouldn't leave them unless it was something important."

It is important. It's my sanity. My soul. My heart.

"You wouldn't understand," she whispered.

"Try me."

She couldn't. She wouldn't. Not ever.

His gaze was suddenly hotly intense and unwavering and Annie was rooted to her spot by the fireplace. His green eyes seemed to travel over her slowly, lingering where the T-shirt didn't quite meet with the waistband of her jeans, exposing her belly just a little. Something flickered inside her. Something that seemed at odds with the usual dynamic of their relationship. Usually she knew what she saw in his gaze…respect, friendship, indifference.

Not this…whatever *this* was.

It was undefinable. Unexpected.

Something told her he was as surprised by the

sudden shift in mood between them as she was. But he still watched her, still allowed his gaze to hone in on her waist and then slowly travel upward, lingering, it seemed, on her breasts.

She swallowed hard, tugging at her shirt. Her nipples hardened instantly, as though her body knew he was observing her in a way that was different, somehow, as though the close confines of the cabin had shifted the dynamic between them on some invisible axis and suddenly they weren't employee and employer...they weren't two people who had been forced into a companionable friendship because of position and familiarity. This was something else. Awareness at a base, primal level. And suddenly her blood was surging through her veins. She wondered if he was as surprised by the moment as she was and hoped that he couldn't see how easily and quickly she reacted to him simply looking at her.

And then hoped, with every ounce of strength she possessed, that David McCall wouldn't realize that she was hopelessly and completely in love with him.

Chapter Three

Of course, it wasn't as though she had woken up one morning and realized that David was the love of her life.

True, she'd always thought he was incredibly attractive, even from those few first meetings a decade ago. But working for David, being a daily part of his life and caring for his children, had allowed her budding awareness to turn into something else. Something more. A deep attraction and a love she couldn't deny.

But her feelings would never be reciprocated. She wasn't his type. He liked women like Rachel, who weren't into commitment. Annie wasn't even sure David registered the fact that she *was* a woman.

They had a good working relationship and she believed they had become friends over the years.

But he would never fall in love with her.

Which is why she had to leave.

The last twelve months had been the hardest. Being around him, watching him date someone else, knowing she was an employee and nothing more—*knowing* she never *would* be anything more—it was all too much to take day in and day out.

There was no other way. It's not like she could or more to the point—*would*—suddenly start acting like some kind of siren and demand David take notice. That wasn't her style. Besides, the dynamic of their relationship had been set from the beginning. He needed a nanny. She wanted a career change. His kids bonded with her quickly and he clearly recognized the value in keeping things between them strictly professional. Even if she *had* been his type, which she wasn't.

He'd briefly dated two other women before Rachel and both had been the same type. Tall and lean and frosty. Not like her. And not like Jayne McCall, either, she thought. Jayne had been pretty in a girl-next-door kind of way. Blond and fair skinned, with freckles and a sweet smile, Jayne had loved her husband, children and flying. Annie had met her a couple of times during visits to town and remembered her as a nice woman, a kind, considerate, lovely person. She'd liked Jayne and often hoped that the other woman would approve of the way she was caring for her children. Of course, she doubted the other woman would be happy if she knew Annie had fallen in love with her husband!

"Annie?" He said her name and jerked her from her trance. "Please tell me what's going on?"

"Stop asking me to explain myself," she said and walked into the kitchen, trying to ignore the way he watched her as she moved, and wondering why he was doing it since she'd never noticed him doing it before.

"What if you get to Texas and this guy turns out to be a crackpot or a serial killer?" David asked, matching her steps.

"Don't be ridiculous," she scoffed and turned on her heel. "He's nothing of the sort."

"How do you know?" he shot back. "What if he's not even this fireman you seem so impressed by? He could be a used-car salesman for all you know."

"Give me *some* credit," she said and rolled her eyes. "We FaceTime, we Skype. I've had several video tours of the fire station where he works," she explained, impatience winding through her blood.

"It could still be a scam," he replied. "And you would care if he couldn't support you."

Annie frowned. "I can support myself. This isn't the Middle Ages."

"Well, what if you move to Texas and marry this guy and have kids and he can't—"

"I'm not rushing out to move to Texas and marry Byron," she said with a sigh.

"You said you wanted to get married," he reminded her.

"Sure, if he's the right guy," she shot back.

"Be sensible, Annie...this is no way to meet someone."

"What do you suggest? Are you now the expert on romance?"

His face darkened. "I don't know how...but not like this. You can't seriously be thinking about meeting this guy?"

She shrugged. "Why can't I? It's part of my plan. I also plan on taking a vacation. Maybe go to Hawaii. Read Brontë novels on the beach. And maybe somewhere in there I'll get married to Byron. But whatever I do, it's none of your business."

"Maybe not," he said and shrugged. "But I feel a certain obligation to make sure you are safe."

"You feel a certain obligation to tell me how to live my life because suddenly it is impacting on yours," she said and scowled. "That's the real reason you're getting so wound up about my leaving."

"I'm not wound up, Annie. I simply want—"

"I know what you want, David," she said, cutting him off as she tugged again at the T-shirt. "You like being organized and having all things going your way, all wrapped up in a neat little balance sheet that you can explain. Well, I can't live like that. I'm not a balance sheet or a number. I'm a woman with real feelings. And like anyone else on the planet sometimes I'm unpredictable and I do things without having a motive or an agenda."

His gaze rolled over her again, this time at a more leisurely pace, making her intensely aware of the sudden lack of space between them. "I'm well aware that you are a woman, Annie."

Could have fooled me...

She shrugged, turning hot all over, despite the fact it was cold and rainy. "Anyway, I think we've covered this subject enough for one day. When do you think we can head back?"

He took his cell phone from his jean pocket, flicked over the screen a few times and then spoke. "According to the weather app, it's going to rain for at least the next couple of hours."

Hours?

I'd rather risk the thunderstorm.

"I think I'll go and check the horses," she said, still tugging at her shirt.

"I'll check them," he said and waved a hand. "No point in you getting wet again now that you're dried off."

She could have sworn that for a moment, just a few seconds, his mouth was curved in a wry sort of smile. A smile that made him look unbelievably sexy. A smile he'd never flashed in her direction before.

I'm imagining things.

She didn't take another breath until he turned and walked out of the cabin.

I have to pull myself together.

David doesn't flash sexy smiles in my direction... not ever.

Annie found the kettle and set it on the stove, then rinsed out Leah's mugs and rummaged through the cupboard for coffee and sugar. The coffee tin was empty and when she found tea bags settled for them, plopping them in the mugs as she waited for the water to boil.

A few minutes later she heard the front door open and close and David was back in the kitchen. "They're fine," he said and plonked his hat on the table. "It's cold in here. We should sit by the fire."

Annie looked at the fire crackling in the hearth and nodded. "I'm making tea."

She knew David didn't really like tea. He was a coffee drinker. But he didn't refuse the mug when she passed it to him. Seconds later they were sitting on the large sofa. It was lumpy and not all that comfortable, but it was better than a kitchen chair.

"I should get some new furniture for this place," he said and stretched out his long legs, holding the mug steady on the arm of the sofa. "Leah still stays here sometimes. It could do with some new drapes and a comfy couch. You can order a few things if you like."

Annie stared at him over the mug. "I'm pretty sure you can do your own shopping."

He shrugged fractionally. "I could, but I hate shopping. You know that."

She did know. In fact, she knew a lot about him. In the four years she'd lived in his home she'd come to know his likes and dislikes and his moods. She knew he liked watching action movies as much as old black-and-white classics. He didn't dance—ever. She knew he liked cherry cola and ham-and-cheese sandwiches. He hated pineapple on pizza and always put extra salt on his fries. He didn't get more than six hours' sleep a night.

He had a scar from having his appendix removed when he was a teenager, and a tattoo of his children's names on his left shoulder. Not that she had seen him totally naked, but over the years there had been occasions when she'd witnessed him coming from the bathroom, a towel slung over his shoulder, his jeans hanging loosely on his hips. Or in the kitchen late at night in pajama bottoms and a tank top. He had an acutely masculine physique and worked out most mornings on the rower or treadmill he had set up in one corner of the huge garage. He had a desk job, after all, so the exercise ensured he didn't spend all of his day sedentary. He even joined her occasionally on her Sunday morning runs if Mittie was able to watch the kids for an hour. He always politely stayed at her pace, and she suspected it was more about catching up about the kids than a serious workout, since she was sure he could have easily outpaced her.

"Leah should do it," she said quietly. "Since she spends the most time here."

"Not a chance," he said and grimaced. "My sister will fill the place with weird-shaped furniture and scented candles."

Annie smiled. Leah *was* known to have eclectic taste in furnishings. "If I get time," she said and shrugged. "I'll look around."

"Didn't you promise to stay for a month?"

She held up two fingers. "Two weeks."

"A month?" he said again, gentler this time, less demanding, more *appealing*.

And Annie felt her resolve slipping. Since she didn't have a job to start, she *could* be a little flexible. "Three weeks. I'll give you an extra week."

He smiled fractionally. "A compromise? It's a start. Although, I still think three weeks isn't nearly long enough to find a replacement. It took me six months to find you."

There was something absurdly intimate about the way he said the words and she colored hotly. *I really need to pull myself together.* Imagining that everything David said to her suddenly had some kind of hidden meaning was ridiculous.

"I'm sure a good placement agency could help you," she said and sipped her tea. "Just tell them what you need and they'll send through applicants with the right qualifications."

"What I need?" he echoed and glanced at her for a moment before focusing his attention toward the fireplace. "Let's see…someone who is reliable, responsible," he said and counted the attributes with his fingers on one large hand. "Trustworthy. Honest. And someone who will cherish my children above anything or anyone else. I don't know…seems unrealistic to expect I can have all that twice in a matter of a few years."

Heat burned behind Annie's eyes and she blinked tears away discreetly. She didn't want to hear praise from him now. It only made her leaving all the more difficult. Which he would know, because David was smart and clearly knew how to push her buttons.

"That person sounds too good to be true," she said flippantly.

"I know," he said, keeping his gaze directly ahead. "But I found her, nonetheless."

"I thought I was the one who did the finding," she reminded him. "I approached you, remember?"

"Thank god," he said and sighed heavily. "After that last drill sergeant, I thought I'd never find you."

It was an odd conversation. Talking about finding one another in that way, to an outside observer, would sound as though they were speaking of lost loves and soul mates—not finding a suitable nanny for his children. But Annie knew in her heart that David would only ever see her as the woman who had stepped into the role of caretaker for his kids.

"I'm sure you'll get someone else who will do a good job," she assured him.

"You know," he said, still not looking at her. "If you want to go to Hawaii, we can go."

"Hawaii?" she repeated incredulously.

"You said you wanted to go to Hawaii. Okay," he said and shrugged a bit. "I'll take you."

"I don't—"

"I haven't been on a real vacation for years and the kids would love it," he said and glanced sideways. "We could ask Nan and Ivan and Leah to come along...make a real family trip of it."

Annie stared at him, her head reeling. *A family trip?* His family. Jayne McCall's family. And Annie would be there as an employee, looking after the kids, doing what she did best.

"No."

"No?" he repeated. "Just like that?"

"Just like that," she replied and sipped more of her tea, wishing for the rain to stop so that she could get up, get out and get away. "But you're right, you should go on a vacation. The kids *would* love it. And I'm sure your new nanny will enjoy a working holiday."

"I didn't mean a working vacation," he said loosely, but Annie saw the way his eyes crinkled at the corners and knew he was tense. "I meant that you could chill out...you know, relax. I could book a couple of suites at one of those big resorts near the beach. I'll look after the kids and you can drink those fancy coconut cocktails with the little umbrellas in them and read your romance novels while you hang out by the pool in a bikini and—"

"Bikini?" She spluttered the word out with a mouthful of tea. "I don't do bikinis."

"Why not?"

Heat suffused her cheeks. "Because…because this is not a bikini kind of body and—"

"You should like your body more," he said quietly and unexpectedly.

Annie didn't dare look at him. It was a very un-David thing to say. She stole a quick glance in his direction. He was staring into the fire, but she noticed a tiny pulse beating in his cheek

He shook his head, almost to himself. "Sorry, I shouldn't have said that, it wasn't appropriate."

Annie tutted. "Stop stressing David, you're the most *appropriate* man I've ever known. You could write a rule book on appropriate behavior."

He turned his head and met her gaze, and something flashed between them. The kind of look she never expected to see in his eyes. For a moment, for one of those flashes of time where the world seemed to stop spinning and everything was focused on only the two of them, Annie could have sworn she registered something that looked a lot like a straight-up physical reaction. Simple chemistry. Awareness. Desire.

No. Impossible.

She'd become a master at hiding her feelings. The queen of denial. He couldn't know she wanted him, craved him, wondered what it would be like to be made love to by him. And even if he did, he certainly wouldn't respond in kind.

She was imagining it. She had to be.

* * *

Strange, David mused as he looked at her, but it took all of his willpower to push back the mental image he had suddenly running riot through his brain. Images of Annie lying on the sand wearing nothing but a tiny, revealing bikini. The idea side-swiped him for a second, and then settled in his blood. The clingy, ill-fitting T-shirt wasn't helping, either. It outlined every dip and curve and left nothing to the imagination. His groin tightened and he shifted uncomfortably, trying to think of something intelligent to say, coming up with nothing. Sure, he wasn't usually much of a talker, but he'd never had trouble talking to Annie. If anything, she was one of the few people he felt genuinely comfortable around. But this feeling...this was different. He wasn't prepared for it. He was...confused.

And he didn't want to be confused about Annie. He didn't want to blur the lines. All he needed was for her to stay and care for his kids. He certainly didn't need to be thinking about her walking along the beach, her lovely curves encased in a bikini top, her hips swinging sexily as she moved. How it might feel to touch her. To run his hand through her honey-colored hair, or bring a lock to his lips...

Goddammit. He cut it off before his imagination could run any further. That was stupid of him. And improper. She *worked* for him. He was her boss. The simple fact she was employed to care for his kids should have waved liked a red flag at that moment. Like it usually did.

So why was it suddenly so hard for him to shut that door?

"The rain's stopped."

Annie's voice pulled him from his unexpected *sex-on-the-brain* trance and he quickly got to his feet. "So it has. I'll turn off the generator and get the horses ready, if you'd like to lock up."

He didn't wait for her reply, didn't dare look at her again. He dumped remains of his tea in the sink, doused the fire—imagining it was his libido that was also getting put out—and left the cottage quickly, taking deep breaths as he made his way to the generator shed. Five minutes later he had the horses ready and was waiting outside for her. She came out, her damp shirt tied around her waist. David ignored her as she put on her boots, but passed her his rain coat when she came down the steps and walked around Star.

"No, I couldn't possibly—"

"Take it," he insisted and pushed the coat into her hands. He sprang into the saddle and waited for her to put on the coat and mount her horse. For a city dweller, Annie had taken to horses liked a seasoned pro. He'd taught her to ride soon after she started working with their family, and admired her skill and determination to be an accomplished rider. "Ready?"

She nodded and pushed her Stetson down low. "Let's go."

The ride back to the stables would take close to an hour as the ground was muddy and slippery and they had to be content with a brisk walk. David stayed in front a few strides, checking the ground for holes or collapsed rabbit burrows. It rained again and he got soaked through, but he ignored it and continued on.

"Annie," he said when he couldn't stand any more of the silence, easing King to a slower pace so she could catch up.

She looked at him. "What?"

David tried to smile, but his jaw felt like granite. "Did you mean what you said earlier? You know, about me being...appropriate?" he asked and then continued on before he lost his nerve. "Because if I've ever behaved in a way that makes you feel as though you're not completely safe, it was never intentional."

She laughed. *Laughed?* When he was torn up inside wondering if he'd ever overstepped. "Believe me, David, you have *always* been a complete gentleman. I know exactly how you feel about me."

She did? Right. The thing was, in that moment, David had no freaking clue.

When they reached the ranch, Rudy was waiting for them and they quickly dismounted.

"Give them a brushdown and a feed," he said and undid the cinch.

He didn't wait for Annie. Didn't want to talk to

her for the moment. He didn't want to dwell on the confusion churning through his head. Didn't want to think about her leaving the ranch, her online fireman boyfriend or what she looked like in a bikini. He headed directly for his bedroom at the rear of the house, ditched his clothes and took a shower, as icy cold as he could stand. He dressed in fresh jeans, a clean shirt and loafers, gathered up the wet clothes and headed for the laundry room.

And bumped head-on into Annie in the doorway.

She yelped in surprise, dropping the basket in her hands. "Sorry," she said and bent to pick it up. She'd clearly showered and changed also, and no longer wore the skin-tight T-shirt. But the loose-fitting pink shirt she had on gaped as she bent over, revealing the soft curve of her breasts and some kind of spandex sports bra that shouldn't have raised his blood pressure a notch, but did. He ignored the inconvenient twitch suddenly rumbling through his body and grabbed the basket so she could continue picking up her clothes. The scent of her perfume, or body lotion, or shampoo or *something*, assailed him instantly and he sucked in a breath, startled by how the mix of vanilla and spice unexpectedly alerted his senses. He'd picked up the same scent countless times before…but in the warm confines of the laundry, it was stronger, more intense, able to work its way under his skin and through his blood.

David cleared his throat and waited, then gently pushed the basket back into her hands.

"The kids…" Her voice trailed off.

"What?"

"They're in the kitchen having a snack, with Mittie. I'm going to play a card game with them."

"It's your day off," he reminded her.

She nodded, but he noticed that her cheeks were ruddy. "I need to talk to them, you know, to tell them I'm leaving."

"We'll do it together."

She looked surprised. "Oh, I thought you'd…"

"What?" he queried. "Leave you to do it alone?" He shook his head. "I don't think that's a good idea. Do you?"

"No. But this morning you said you weren't going to play bad cop."

"I was angry this morning," he admitted quietly.

She look startled by his candor. "And now?"

Now I'm just confused.

"I just want to protect my kids, Annie. That's *my* job."

Her eyes glistened, like she was fighting back emotion. Whatever was going on between them, he didn't like to think she was upset, even if she *had* turned his world upside down.

"Spend whatever time you need with the kids," he said, secretly wanting nothing more than to get away from her. "I'll join you soon."

She bit her lower lip, and he wondered for a moment if she wanted to ask him something, but she didn't.

She disappeared, but David stayed in the laundry room for a moment, loading the washing machine, then slamming the door harder than necessary. He rested his hands on the machine and took a long breath, exhaling heavily. *Get a grip.* He couldn't believe how complicated things had become in a matter of hours. Yesterday his life was perfectly normal. He had routine. He knew what to expect. Everything was okay in his world. But Annie had blown that routine spectacularly out of the water.

David was tempted to lock himself in his office for an hour or so to help get the chaos out of his head. Work always cleared his thoughts. After Jayne and his mom had died, it was work that got him through the tough days. That, and stepping up to be both mother and father to his kids. And of course, soon after, there was Annie. Like an angel, she'd picked up the scattered pieces and brought calm to the chaos.

David sighed. Hiding in his office wasn't the answer. Annie planned on telling the kids and he needed to be there when she did. He stretched his back as his gut rumbled. The day had been so dramatic he'd forgotten to eat. He left the laundry and walked to the kitchen, finding his kids at the table, playing a game of Go Fish with Annie. She looked up when he entered the room, her lovely mouth curling into a smile at the edges.

Lovely mouth?

Where on earth did *that* come from?

David shook his head, moved around the countertop and opened the refrigerator, acutely aware that she was watching his every move, but trying to look as though she wasn't.

"Where's Mittie?" he asked.

"In her room," Annie replied. "She said she had an email to send to her travel agent."

"Did you tell her…" His voice trailed off and he shrugged lightly.

"Yes."

"Daddy," Scarlett said and turned, grinning in the way that always made David's heart flip over. "Jasper doesn't play fair."

Annie laughed softly and the sound echoed around the room. Had he ever noticed before how sweet and husky her laugh was? He met her gaze, half smiled for a second and then stopped rummaging through the refrigerator for a snack. His daughter didn't quite know the rules of the game, but she certainly knew when her brother was cheating.

"Jasper," he said with one brow raised. "No cheating, okay, sport?"

Jasper shrugged and widened his eyes innocently. "Sure, Dad."

David returned to the refrigerator and spotted a leftover serving of lasagna. He unwrapped the dish, then popped it into the microwave. Before he pressed the timer, Annie spoke.

"Ah, Jasper… Scarlett," she said quietly, "there's something I need to tell you."

David noticed that her hands were pressed flat on the table. She was nervous and he saw real pain in her expression. He tried being mad at her and failed. The truth was, she'd given far more than she'd taken over the years. He came around the counter, perched on the edge of a stool and waited for her to speak.

"I'm going away soon," she explained simply, her voice almost cracking. "In a few weeks. Which means I won't be your nanny anymore."

David watched as she swallowed hard after each long breath. And he knew, in that moment, how hard it was for her.

No one said anything for several seconds. Scarlett was fiddling with her cards and he noticed that Jasper was tugging on his bottom lip with his teeth.

"So, you won't be taking care of us?" his son asked quietly, his concentration focused on the cards in his hand.

Annie nodded and spoke gently. "No, sweetie, I won't. You'll have a new nanny who will look after you."

His son still didn't look up. "Just not you?"

Scarlett got off her chair and stood beside Annie. "But I don't want a new nanny."

Annie grasped his daughter's hand gently. "I know you don't and it'll be hard at first. For all of us," she added and glanced up at him.

David saw his daughter's expression crumble and his heart just about broke. His kids understood. They knew what Annie's departure would mean to them. They knew how lost they would all be.

"I don't want you to leave," Scarlett said, her bottom lip wobbling. "I want you to stay. I want—"

"Scarlett," David said and moved to the table, reaching for his daughter when the tears in her eyes became too much to bear. "It'll be okay, honey," he said and hauled her into his arms. "I promise."

She hugged him, dropping her face into his shoulder, hiccuping a couple of times. He noticed she was still holding the cards tightly in her small hand. "How about you finish your game?" he suggested and sat her back down at the table.

Scarlett nodded and let out a shuddering beath. "Okay, Daddy."

David met Annie's gaze, noticing how bright her eyes shone, and suspected she was barely hanging on to her emotions. He managed a tight smile. Trying to offer comfort, even though she'd turned his world upside down.

"You okay, buddy?" he asked his son and ruffled his hair.

Jasper nodded, blinking hard. "Will you play cards with us, Dad?"

He looked at Jasper's strained expression and quickly sat. As much as he, too, was confused by Annie's decision, he wouldn't show it in front of his children. "Sure. Deal me in."

They played a round and he ignored the tense silence. But by the second round Jasper tossed his cards into the middle of the table and said he'd had enough and quickly left the room.

"Should I go to him?" Annie asked, half rising.

David got to his feet, noticing how Scarlett was once again holding Annie's hand. "I'll do it."

He found Jasper in his room, sitting in a chair by his fish tank. He remained by the door for a moment, remembering how he'd had to have the hard conversation about Jayne's death over four years earlier. Jasper had been so young, and it had taken time for the reality of losing his mom to truly sink in. For the first few days he'd cried a lot, and then, suddenly, he stopped, and never appeared to cry again. David wondered if he was right in letting Jasper keep his pain dammed up at such a young age. But he'd never wanted to force his son to talk about his mother or the accident. He figured he would, when he was ready.

"Hey, sport," he said, resting a shoulder against the door frame. "Are you okay?"

Jasper nodded and continued to stare into the tank.

"If you want to talk, I'm here to listen."

"I know, Dad. But I don't feel like talking right now."

They were so alike, he thought and sighed. David didn't like talking much about feelings, either.

He felt a small hand curl into his own and spotted Scarlett at his side. "Hey there."

"Daddy," she said, her eyes glistening. "I'm sad.

But Annie looks sad, too. You should go and cheer her up."

David's insides clenched. "I thought I'd hang out with you guys for a while."

"I wanna watch the fish with Jasper," she announced and quickly moved into the room and plonked herself on the floor, lotus-style, in front of the tank.

David looked at his children and his heart tightened in his chest. As much as he hated admitting it, sometimes it was impossible to protect them from the world.

"How about we go and take another look at the kittens later?" he suggested. "Before it gets dark?"

"Yay!" Scarlett said, clearly a little happier at the idea.

Jasper nodded, and David left his kids sitting together, watching the fish, and headed back to the kitchen.

"Is Jasper okay?" Annie asked the moment David crossed the threshold. She was still sitting at the table, wringing her hands.

He nodded and moved around the counter, flicking on the microwave. "He's okay. But quiet. You know how he gets."

She sighed. "I'll talk to him later. I know it's the weekend, but I could tuck him into bed tonight."

David rested his behind on the counter. "I should probably tuck the kids in every night from now on, don't you think? You know, get them used to not—"

"Having me around?" she said, cutting him off. "I suppose so."

He looked at her, noticing how huge her eyes looked in her face. "Scarlett said you needed cheering up?"

She made a humorless sound. "That was harder than I ever imagined it might be. But since you're so angry with me," she reminded him with a wry expression, "I'm not sure you're the person for the job."

"I'm not angry," he replied. "I mean, I was this morning. But it was more surprise than anything else. Now I'm just...confused."

She stared at him, her eyes widening even further.

The microwave is beeping."

He'd forgotten all about the lasagna. He took the leftovers from the microwave, held the dish in a tea towel, grabbed two forks from the cutlery drawer and headed back to the table.

"Hungry?" he asked and passed her a fork.

She took the utensil and they sat for a while, snacking on the leftovers, and the mood between them was oddly calm. As though it could have been any day, any time. Not the day she'd decided to walk out of his life.

Their lives, he reminded himself firmly.

"I'm sorry they're hurting," she said softly.

David's throat tightened. "Scarlett and Jasper don't want to lose you."

She dipped the fork into the dish. "I know."

"Neither do I."

She stilled. "I know that, too."

David reached out and grasped her hand, holding her steady. For a moment he thought she might pull away, but she didn't. She remained still, slowly meeting his gaze.

There were no rings on her fingers. But there would be, one day, if the fireman got his way. The idea bugged him so much he could barely sit still in the chair. Of course, she could do what she liked. She was a free agent. But the idea that she would consider doing something so impulsive seemed completely at odds with the reliable, responsible woman he'd come to know and care about over the past few years.

"Annie?"

Her throat convulsed a little and he watched, fascinated by how long and smooth her neck was. How had he never noticed that before? Or the brilliantly blue shade of her eyes. Or how sharply arched her brows were, and how it created a stunning combination.

"Yes?"

He took a long breath, and gently rubbed her palm with his thumb. "What can I do to make this right?"

Chapter Four

Fall in love with me...

Of course, she didn't say that. She wouldn't, ever. Annie quickly pulled her hand from his. They shouldn't be holding hands. That was against the rules. "I want you to *stop* asking me what you can do," she replied. "There's nothing to do, David. I'm leaving, so you'll just have to get used to the idea."

But she knew he wouldn't. She knew he would keep asking, keep pushing, keep trying to work out a way to get her to change her mind. As calm and reserved as he was, she knew he could be stubborn and hardnosed when he wanted to get his own way.

He pushed back his chair and got to his feet. "This isn't like you, Annie."

"I know you might be astounded that I've suddenly developed a sense of initiative," she said and stood. "But this *is* me, David. And frankly, I'm surprised a smart guy like you didn't see this coming. Despite how much I care about the kids, you really can't expect me to stay forever. I do need my own life at some point. Why can't you understand that?"

"Who says you can't have both?" he shot back irritably. "I mean, I haven't stopped you from having a life, Annie. I've never stopped you from dating or having a boyfriend, or lover, or fiancé or even a husband. If that's what you want, go and find one. It doesn't have to change the fact you work here. Most people manage to work and have a personal life. And they don't make plans to run halfway across the country to be with someone they've never met."

"This isn't just about Byron," she retorted and noticed how he winced, as though the mention of the other man riled him in some way. "I said I wanted a life...one that doesn't revolve around my job." *Or you*.

"What will you do for money?" he asked bluntly.

"I have savings," she replied. "And I'll get another job." Annie saw the cynicism in his expression. "You can be really...insensitive...do you know that?"

His mouth curved. It made him look sexier, if that was possible. And Annie longed to *not* think about him that way. She tried to shift her gaze and failed. Because David had some kind of pull over her that was impossible to deny.

"I'm only trying to understand," he said evenly. "You have to admit, this kind of came out of left field. I had no idea you were so unhappy."

Because you don't see me...

"Well, I am," she said and then sighed.

He took a moment before responding and when he did he sounded weary and resigned. "I guess I'll place an ad with a job-placement agency. Maybe we could do the interviews together," he suggested. "How does that sound?"

It sounded like a terrible idea. The last thing Annie wanted to do was recruit her own replacement. She glared at him, fighting back her instinct to huff. "Sure, whatever."

David looked skeptical by her quick agreement. "All right, I'll make sure we have a few interviews set up next week."

"Fine."

He took the dishes to the sink and cleaned up. Annie admired the way he was so self-sufficient. He had a housekeeper that came once a week, and Annie, but he still did chores around the house when he was home. When Mittie was at the ranch she did most of the cooking, but his grandmother lived her own life, having many friends across the globe, and usually traveled for half the year. Annie cooked too, but she wasn't as adventurous as Mittie, who'd picked up her culinary skills on her travels through Europe and Asia.

Annie got up and left the kitchen, heading for her

own rooms, finding peace and solitude amongst the familiarity of her own things, her own *space*. The truth was, Annie loved the ranch and the people in it. The problem was, David would *never* love her in return. And to live at the ranch, to be a part of things, but always apart, was not how she wanted to live the rest of her life. Of course, it wasn't his fault. It was her own. He had no clue how she felt, and she couldn't force him to suddenly have feelings for her.

She settled herself on the sofa and grabbed her cell phone to call her sister. Tess answered on the fourth ring and Annie could hear her ten-month-old nephew chattering in the background.

"His favorite word is *Dada* at the moment," her sister said and chuckled. "Mitch thinks it's wonderful, of course. So, how did it go?"

Tess knew David wouldn't be happy that Annie was resigning from her job. "As well as expected."

"You told the kids?"

Annie's insides crunched. Telling Jasper and Scarlett she was leaving was one of the hardest things she'd ever done. Guilt, deep and gut-wrenching, pressed down heavily on her shoulders.

"Yes, I told them," she said.

"And how did David react?" Tess prompted.

"Offered me a raise and a trip to Hawaii," she said stiffly.

Tess sighed. "Well, you knew he wouldn't be happy about it. It's a big change for the kids. And for him," her sister added.

"He'll get used to it."

"Did you tell him why?" Tess asked.

"I told him I wanted to move on with my life."

"And did you tell him about the fireman?" her sister asked.

Annie's cheeks heated. "A little. He thinks I'm crazy."

Tess laughed. "Plenty of people find love online. Only…"

"Only?" she prompted.

"They're not usually in love with someone else. Maybe you should just lay it out and see what happens. Tell David how you feel and go from there."

"I can't," she replied quickly. "It's too humiliating."

"Perhaps he feels the same way."

Annie laughed without humor. "Oh, please, David only sees me as a caretaker for his kids. I'm the nanny, Tess. That's all."

"He'll be lost without you."

"He'll survive," she corrected.

They chatted for a while and when she ended the call, Annie felt a little better. Still, she couldn't get David out of her thoughts. She didn't want to relive the painful moments of the day, yet couldn't help thinking about what had transpired down by the river. There had been an intensity about their interaction—something she hadn't experienced before. There had been tension, too. But, nothing unusual about that. She'd butted heads with David more times than she could remember over the years. If he wanted a nanny who was compliant and did everything he said, he would be greatly disappointed.

She sighed, thinking about her life, wondering how it had come to this point. Long ago, when she was in college and dreaming of her future, she'd imagined a much different scenario. A home of her own, a man who loved her and children to raise. Everyday things, she'd believed at the time.

Now, those dreams seemed so far away. Perhaps it was watching her sister get her happily-ever-after that had forced her hand and made her admit she needed to make some changes. To find her own happy ending. Whatever the reason, Annie knew it was time she moved on, away from David McCall. Otherwise her heart would never heal.

David rolled out of bed the following morning and planted his feet on the floor, pressing a hand to his temple. The three belts of bourbon he'd had the night before were an attempt to erase the idea of Annie leaving from his thoughts—instead, all he'd done was end up with a headache. He wasn't much of a drinker and generally preferred a clear head, but last night, after the kids were in bed and Annie and his grandmother had retired for the night, he'd sat in the living room and contemplated his situation.

But nothing made sense.

Not only Annie's resignation, but how it made him feel. Primarily, the acute sense of something that felt a lot like…*abandonment*. It was irrational, of course, for him to think that. He knew it logically. The problem was, in the last twenty-four hours, his usual logic seemed to have deserted him.

David spent half an hour on the rowing machine and then took a shower to clear his thoughts, dressed in jeans and black shirt and headed for the kitchen. Mittie was behind the counter and she gave him a quizzical look when he perched on the edge of a counter stool.

"Rough night?" she asked.

David shrugged. "You know Annie quit yesterday."

His grandmother's expression softened. "Do you know why?"

"She wants to move on. She wants… I guess she wants a different life."

Mittie smiled. "Can't really blame her, I suppose."

David wasn't sure he agreed. "I've never stopped her from having her own life. And she's planning on running away to Texas with some guy she's *never* met, did she tell you that?"

His grandmother raised a brow. "That's not exactly what she said."

"Isn't it?" he said, a bitter taste forming in his mouth. "She met some guy online, some fireman, and thinks he might be the love of her life. She wants to get married and run off into the sunset with him."

"That doesn't sound so bad," Mittie said and grinned.

David moaned. "Please don't encourage her to be irresponsible."

"Why would I do that?" she queried, still grinning.

"Because you're a hopeless romantic who watches way too many sappy movies."

Mittie made a disapproving face. "You're about as romantic as an old shoe. Sometimes I wonder how you ever were your father's son. He was such a romantic. He courted your mother the old-fashioned way, with flowers and candy and he even sang to her—of course they were young, still more or less teenagers, so perhaps that had something to do with it. But I remember how your grandfather used to write me the most romantic poetry." She sighed and smiled. "You're missing that gene. However did you get Jayne to marry you?"

"Jayne was as sensible and pragmatic as I am," David replied and shook his head, remembering the small wedding at the courthouse, her insistence that flowers were a waste of money and their reception afterward at a local restaurant. "And I'm not averse to romance, but I don't see anything romantic in running off to god knows where to meet someone who could potentially be a serial killer. Annie should show more sense."

"There's more to life than being sensible, David. You used to know that."

Maybe he had. Once, long ago. Before he'd lost everything.

"I don't see how racing off with some guy she's never met constitutes romance. The fact is, I'm concerned for her safety."

Mittie's brows rose higher. "Is that what it is?"

David wasn't sure what he heard in her query. "Of course. What else?"

"She's turning your world upside down."

"You're right, she is," he agreed, irritation weaving through his chest when he remembered the fact. "The kids need her and she's abandoning them."

And me.

"That's correct," Mittie said gently. "She *is* needed here. Although I'm not sure you fully comprehend why."

David gaped at his grandmother. "What does *that* mean?"

"You're a smart boy," she said and then paused as Scarlett came running into the room. "I'm sure you'll figure it out."

David hugged his daughter and was just about to settle her at the table for breakfast when Annie walked into the room, dressed in yoga pants, a Jo-Jo's Pizza T-shirt, clearly seeking coffee. When he caught her gaze, she quickly turned toward his grandmother and she said something about needing sugar.

"Not running this morning?" he asked.

She shrugged one shoulder. "I wasn't in the mood," she said and grabbed the sugar bowl Mittie passed to her. "Thank you," Annie said and ruffled the top of Scarlett's head. "Morning, sweetie."

His little girl's face beamed. "Can we play princesses today, Annie?"

"It's Annie's day off today, remember?" he reminded his daughter, and then hoped *he* didn't get stuck with the princess-playtime gig because he really didn't look so great in a tiara.

Which was obviously what Annie was thinking, because she glanced at him and grinned. "How about this afternoon," she said and turned her attention to Scarlett.

It was her day off, but David knew she rarely said no to his daughter. And she wasn't likely to do so now, particularly since she was leaving. She looked back his way. "I'm going to the Triple C this morning to see Tess and the baby. Why don't I take her with me? Unless you have plans with her and Jasper of your own today?"

"Nothing I can't change," he replied,

David shot a look toward his curiously staring grandmother, then met Annie's gaze. "Better still, I'll come with you, since I need to catch up with Mitch about something," he suggested and shrugged lightly. "And we can bring Jasper, too."

The tiny line between her brows furrowed a little, but she nodded. "Okay."

"Tenish work for you?"

"Sure. See you then," she said and turned on her heel.

Once she was gone, David moved behind the counter and grabbed a cereal bowl for his daughter. He knew Mittie was watching him and felt her scrutiny down to the soles of his feet.

"What?" he said, not looking at her.

"You remember that I have that Alaskan cruise coming up?" she reminded him. "So I won't be here for a month."

He looked at the calendar on the refrigerator. Mittie highlighted the days and weeks she vacationed so he could keep track of her movements. As much as he was grateful for the way she helped around the place when she was at the ranch, she wasn't the sort who would settle for an ordinary life. Mittie loved to travel and he supported her vacationing and need to see the world.

"I remember."

"You need to fix this," she said quietly. "Or else this family will be torn apart."

"I know that," he said, equally as quiet. "The kids adore Annie… I don't know how I'm supposed to replace her in three weeks."

"You can't," his grandmother said bluntly. "So, think of something to make her stay."

"I offered her a raise and a paid vacation and she pretty much told me to go to hell. It's not money she wants."

Mittie raised a quizzical brow. "No, David. She wants a husband. And a family."

David stilled instantly. "What exactly are you suggesting?"

"A possible solution."

He laughed when he realized what she meant. "Be serious. Annie works for me. Our relationship is strictly professional and I—"

"If you say so."

David didn't miss the curious twinkle in his grandmother's eyes. But her insinuation that *he* was the solution was way off base. The idea of anything happening with Annie was out of the question.

Or was it?

They didn't think about each other that way.

Or did they?

Sure, she was beautiful. And yeah, he wasn't made of stone—he tried to maintain that professional distance, but even he couldn't help but take notice of her looks occasionally. But anything further was off the table.

So, yes, perhaps when they were at the cottage yesterday there was *something* stirring that he couldn't completely dismiss. Something that had kept him awake for the better part of the night, wondering *what if... what if he'd completely missed a moment...* But that was yesterday. And today was a different story. Today he had to think of a way to get her to stay that didn't include some crazy notion his grandmother alluded to.

He spent the next couple of hours with the kids, getting them dressed for their outing. Jasper was quieter than usual, but David didn't press him to talk. When his son was ready, he would open up, that was Jasper's way. Much like his own, he suspected. They waited for Annie by his BMW and she came out of the house at a minute after ten, her hair down, her jean-clad hips swaying as she walked, her jacket accentuating her curves.

Whoa.

David frowned, shook his head and concentrated on getting the kids buckled into their seats in the back of the SUV. He refused to spare another thought for the way Annie looked. Until she got into the front seat and her fragrance hit his senses like a freight train.

It was going to be a long ride...

The drive to the Triple C ranch was a relatively short one—just twenty minutes—and they had done it together countless times, but never with so much thick tension between them. Once he turned the car into the long driveway he could almost feel her sense of relief, as though she couldn't wait to be away from him. When he pulled up and stopped the car, Jasper was out in a flash, while Scarlett waited to be unbuckled from her booster seat.

David spotted Mitch striding across the yard from the stables, his swagger that of the quintessential cowboy. His cousin was also his closest friend. He'd raised his five siblings after their father, Billie-Jack, had run out on them, and Mitch had been there for him when Jayne and his mom died, even though he'd been going through his divorce from Tess at the time. It was unbelievable, really, that he and Tess had found their way back to one another after so much grief and loss.

He noticed that Annie was out of the car and was walking up to the house with Scarlett's hand clutched in her own, while Jasper headed for his uncle. Well, technically, his son's second cousin, but they would always regard each other's kids as nieces and nephews. A couple of dogs raced around the yard and quickly captured Jasper's attention.

Mitch tilted his Stetson. "Mornin'," he said and grinned. "Don't think I need to ask how you are, right?"

David glanced in Annie's direction as she headed up the steps and disappeared into the big house. "I take it you've heard?"

His cousin nodded. "She called Tess yesterday."

David kept one eye on his son, who was still petting the dogs. "Of course. Did Tess tell you about the fireman Annie plans on running off with?"

Mitch laughed and slapped him across the back. "Looks like you're screwed then. I mean, how do you compete with that?"

David frowned. What was with everyone today? First his grandmother, now Mitch? "I don't plan on competing with anyone. She wants to leave so she can get married. Probably to this..." he gestured in frustration "...stranger."

Mitch grinned. "That might be a little premature. She's never actually met this guy, right?"

He shrugged. "Not yet, but they've been *corresponding* for months, apparently. I'm just as confused by the whole thing as you are. Maybe Tess can talk some sense into her."

"Don't count on it," Mitch replied. "My wife thinks it's romantic and has volunteered to be with Annie when she meets this guy."

David tossed his hands in the air. "Great! Has everyone lost their minds in the last twenty-four hours?"

"Possibly," Mitch said and laughed again. "Tess said her sister has been thinking about it for some time."

"Nice to be told."

"You can be a hard-ass," Mitch said and grinned. "Maybe she avoided telling you because she knew you wouldn't listen rationally."

"I'm rational," David corrected.

"When it suits you," Mitch supplied. "And you were never going to be rational about this."

"Why do you say that?"

Mitch rolled his eyes. "Because, my friend, you can't live without her."

David heard truth in the other man's words, but didn't want to consider it...didn't want to question what it meant.

"What?" he said, exasperated.

"Put it this way," Mitch said quietly and rested his behind on the hood of the SUV. "You rely on Annie completely…she's been the one constant in your life since you lost Jayne and your mom, hasn't she?"

David shrugged. "I…well…yes, I guess so."

"So, it makes perfect sense that you didn't see this coming, because you weren't looking for it."

"Because I'm so wrapped up in myself, you mean?" he suggested sarcastically, not liking the way the words sounded. "Thanks for setting me straight."

Mitch shook his head. "There it is…that annoying arrogance. None of us are perfect—ask my wife. She'll tell you what a pain in the ass I am. Genetic dysfunction perhaps," he said and laughed. "The thing is, you have to make Annie want to stay *more* than she wants to leave—and this guy in Texas you mentioned seems like all the motivation she needs to bail and race off looking for what she wants. Or maybe it's just what she *thinks* she wants."

David scowled. "You're not helping."

"Sure I am," Mitch flipped back. "Simply work out what she wants more than this guy."

"I do know. She wants to get married and have kids. Want to hear something funny—Mittie suggested that *I* should, you know, marry her," he said humorlessly.

Mitch shrugged and offered a lopsided grin. "It's not such a bad idea."

"It was a joke," David said and shook his head. "Annie and I don't…we don't think about each other that way."

Except as David said the words, he felt something crumble inside him. Because though it sounded like the truth—the same truth he'd believed for years—somehow, it didn't sit right. It didn't make sense. And he had no idea why his beliefs had shifted so suddenly. The idea of losing Annie rocked the very foundations of his life and Mitch was right—he didn't want to lose her. But marriage? How could they? It wasn't logical, was it?

"You'd rather watch as she marries someone else?"

David jerked his attention back to his cousin. "What?"

"Because that's what will happen," Mitch said bluntly. "Maybe it won't be this guy, but it will be someone, one day. And since you're in a position to do something about it, then *do* something about it. The fact is, Jayne wouldn't want you to be alone."

David knew that. But the truth was, he didn't feel alone. He had his family, his kids. *And Annie.* He ignored the twitch in his gut. "Marriage isn't the answer."

Mitch shrugged. "And it won't be," his cousin said flatly. "Not while you're still wearing your wedding ring."

David glanced down at the narrow band on his left hand. Most days he forgot it was there.

Anyway, Annie didn't want him in that way. She wanted her fireman, online love. Changing the rules and the dynamic of their relationship would be plain stupid.

And he wasn't stupid. He might be a hard-ass. He might be arrogant. He might be a whole lot of things...but he wasn't about to start making any kind of fool of himself in a desperate attempt to get her to stay. Not a chance.

"He's so beautiful, Tess," Annie said as she rocked her sleeping nephew in her arms, staring lovingly at his perfect little face.

Tess sighed and sat on the opposite sofa in the huge living room. "I know. Some days I can't believe how lucky I am, considering everything that happened."

Annie met her sister's gaze. Years ago, the first time around that she'd married Mitch, Tess had endured several failed pregnancies. It was why her marriage to Mitch had ended. But now she had her son and the devotion of the only man she'd ever loved. Of course, Annie was a little envious, but she was also genuinely happy for her sister. And she wanted that same happiness for herself—including a husband and a baby. Her clock was ticking. And her life needed to change if she was going to get what she wanted.

"Mitch is a lucky man. I can't imagine how good

it must feel spending each day with the person you love most in the world," she said and sighed.

Tess raised a brow. "Can't you?"

Annie's cheeks heated. She knew what Tess meant. "It's not the same thing."

Her sister regarded her with gentle understanding. "I still think you should lay it all out. What have you got to lose?"

"You mean besides complete humiliation? And my pride?"

"That's your emotions talking," Tess said softly.

"Exactly," she replied and smiled. "I'm a sucker for them. That's what got me into this mess."

"You fell in love," Tess reminded her.

"And now I have to fall *out* of love," she said quietly, looking at Scarlett, who sat on the rug in front of the fireplace, playing with a couple of Charlie's stuffed toys. "No problem."

Tess offered a gentle nod. "But it's not just one person you have to fall out of love with, is it?" Tess asked intuitively.

Annie swallowed the lump burning her throat. Her heart was breaking merely *thinking* about leaving Scarlett and Jasper—imagining how she'd be when she actually left, didn't bear considering—unless she wanted to fall into a heap.

She looked at the photographs on the mantel—generations of Culhanes, including a recent photograph of the entire family, taken at Mitch and Tess's wedding. Annie found herself in the picture, holding

Scarlett, standing beside David. To an outsider, it would look as though they were very much a family unit. But looks were deceiving. True, the Culhanes had always treated her like family, and she genuinely liked them, particularly Mitch's sister Ellie. And since her good friend Abby had recently married Mitch's younger brother Jake, the connection with them all had become even stronger. Yes, she was one of them now, while she worked for David and lived in Cedar River. But afterwards, when she was replaced by another nanny, she wondered if that would change. Would she be regarded as Tess's stepsister and nothing more? The memory of her would fade. Particularly if she moved away to somewhere like Texas.

Byron. She'd barely spared him a thought in the last twenty-four hours. He'd texted her that morning and she'd held off responding. She wasn't sure why. Perhaps because her emotions were in such turmoil and she didn't want to add any fuel to her already fractured feelings.

"Byron's asking to meet," she said, keeping her voice low so that Scarlett wouldn't pick up on the strain in her tone.

"Are you having second thoughts?"

She shrugged. "Second and third and fourth," she admitted. "I just want to be sure I'm doing the right thing."

"I guess there are no guarantees in any relationship,' Tess added. "But you'll never know unless you take the chance."

"So," she queried, her voice quiet. "You think I should do it?"

"You know what I think," Tess replied gently.

Tell David how she felt...

"I can't," she whispered.

Tess got to her feet. "I'm here for you, whatever you decide. And now I think I'll go and make coffee for you and tea for me," her sister said and then called Scarlett's name, asking her if she wanted milk and cookies.

Scarlett was on her feet in a microsecond and Annie continued to cradle Charlie after they left the room. Alone, with her thoughts and the sleepy baby in her arms, Annie's sense of longing became acute.

Particularly when David came into the room a few minutes later. Of course, he'd seen her hold a baby before. Scarlett had been a little over six months old when she'd arrived at the ranch. But something had changed between them in the last twenty-four hours; their regard for one another, their entire *relationship*, had undergone some sort of dramatic shift. Her announcement that she was quitting had clearly made things difficult and tense between them.

"I remember when Jasper was born," he said and came farther into the room, standing behind the sofa. "I spent the first few months terrified I was going to drop him, or forget to feed him." He smiled a little and looked at the baby, then returned his gaze to hers. "I'd relaxed a bit by the time Scarlett came along. Jayne was way more relaxed about the whole thing. Mothering instinct, maybe," he said and then chuckled. "Or does that make me sound like a sexist jerk?"

Annie couldn't help herself and smiled in return. He had a sexy laugh and she had never been immune. "Not really. I understand what you mean."

"Jayne was a good mom," he said softly. "You will be, too," he added. "I mean, when you…"

"When I *finally* get to have a child of my own?"

He immediately looked uncomfortable. "I didn't mean it like that. I only meant—"

"It's okay," she said and sighed. "I'm being overly sensitive. Forget about it."

"He's a cute kid," he said and sat down in the sofa opposite.

"All babies are cute."

He didn't disagree. Instead, he sat back in the chair, watching her. "So, this fireman," he said suddenly and unexpectedly. "Does he want kids?"

Annie met his gaze. "Yes," she replied and glanced briefly toward the door. "Is Jasper with Mitch?"

He nodded. "Mitch is showing him the new foal that was born last night." He tapped his fingers on the arm of the chair. "So…yeah…about this fireman…has he asked you to marry him?"

Annie gaped at him. "Ah...no. We've never met, remember."

"But you've talked about marriage?"

She was surprised by his questions and didn't bother to hide the fact. "In a vague kind of way," she replied, her cheeks burning beneath his glittering gaze. "You know, the way people generally talk about marriage and relationships."

"We've lived together for four years and the subject of marriage has never come up."

Annie bit back the startled gasp that rose in her throat. "I don't know what –"

"You've never said you wanted to get married," he remarked, still tapping his fingers.

"Wanting marriage and babies isn't exactly the kind of conversation someone has with their employer."

He stopped tapping, looking serious through his glasses. "I've always thought we were friends."

Annie almost laughed out loud. If she told him how much she wanted him out of the *employer-zone* and into the *lover-zone*, he'd run a mile.

"We are, David," she said quietly and firmly. "So, please, be my friend. Just support my decision."

As painful as it was, Annie knew leaving was the right thing to do.

For all their sakes.

Sunday night was game night – his sister usually dropped by, bringing Ivan, her face painting gear and treats for the kids. David always enjoyed the family get-togethers, particularly when Mittie was home. He and Ivan would watch sport on the big TV in the rumpus room, while their grandmother made snacks and his sister painted the kid's faces. And then they would all sit around the table in the kitchen, eat copious amounts of popcorn and play cards or Scrabble. It was tradition. Most times, Annie would join in, unless she was visiting Tess. But she was painfully absent that evening. And neither Jasper or Scarlett were in their usual playful mood.

"What's with the gloomy faces?" Ivan asked both kids as he peered over his cards.

Jasper shrugged and David winced when he saw the unhappiness in his son's face when he spoke. "Annie's going away."

"Daddy," Scarlett said once her brother's words were out. "Doesn't Annie like us anymore?"

David's chest tightened and he gently touched his daughter's cheek. "Of course she does, honey."

"It'll be hard to replace that girl," Ivan said and raised a brow.

"Impossible," Leah added.

"I thought we were playing cards," David said, eager to shift the somber mood and change the subject. He'd spent the better part of two days thinking about Annie – it was time he got his mind on other things.

Scarlett lasted another half an hour before her

eyes began to droop and David hauled her into his arms and made a quick stop at the bathroom to remove the face paint before he changed her into her pajamas and tucked her into bed. She was more restless than usual and took about ten minutes to settle her with a night light and a page from her favorite story book.

"Daddy," she said as he kissed her forehead. "You'll never leave us, will you?"

They were some of the most painful words he had ever heard and his already tight chest constricted even further. His children had already lost so much. "No," he assured her. "I'll never leave you or Jasper."

Her expression relaxed and she closed her sleepy eyes. "I love you, Daddy."

David could barely swallow the emotion burning his throat. "I love you too, honey. Goodnight, and sweet dreams."

He left the door ajar, quickly heading down the hall and discovered Jasper brushing his teeth in the bathroom.

"Everything okay?"

His son nodded and plopped his toothbrush in the cup. "I'm not a baby," he announced. "I don't need tucking in."

"I know," David assured him. "I thought you might want to talk about things."

Jasper shook his head. "I was thinking I could save up my allowance," he said, so matter-of-factly as they walked down the hallway and into his son's room. "And give it to Annie. She might stay if she got more money for looking after us."

David stilled, his insides crunching, his heart aching for his child who was trying to find logic amidst his confusion. He waited until Jasper was in bed before he responded. "It's not about money. It's about grown-up things. And we'll all be fine, I promise."

He didn't look as reassured as his sister, but he nodded. "Goodnight, Dad."

David said goodnight and left the room, making his way back to the kitchen. He glanced toward the door that led to Annie's rooms. *Out of bounds.* Damn, he really wanted to talk to her, to try and make her see what her leaving was doing to his children. But he wasn't about to lay on a guilt trip. He hesitated for a second and then returned to the kitchen. Coffee was brewing and the cards were packed away, and other than his kids, the three people he loved most in the world were all staring at him as he entered the room.

He raised his hands. "I don't want a lecture, okay. I know my kids are hurting."

"Isn't there something you can do?" Leah implored.

David glanced at Mittie and saw the suggestion in his grandmother's eyes. "Nothing that Annie would agree to," he said quietly. "Or that I'm prepared to do."

"What does that mean?" his sister shot back.

David ran a hand through his hair. "Nothing. How about we call it a night?"

They all agreed and within minutes Leah and their dad left and Mittie headed to her room. David remained where he was, leaning against the counter top, dreading the headache that was pounding at his temples. He pulled off his glasses, closed his eyes and pressed two fingers to the bridge of his nose.

"Are you okay?"

He opened his eyes and spotted Annie by the doorway. She wore baggy pink sweats he'd probably seen countless times, but he couldn't remember ever thinking how naturally beautiful she looked with her lovely hair down around her shoulders.

"Headache," he replied.

She moved into the kitchen, opened the pantry and withdrew the small locked medicine box from the top shelf. Seconds later she placed aspirin and a glass of water in front of him.

"Be a good boy and take the medicine," she said, and waited until he took the pills.

He did as she instructed. "You missed family night," he remarked, finishing off the water.

"I had things to do."

"Skyping with the fireman?"

Her eyes widened and he figured she had every reason to look stunned by his question – because he had just startled himself. And he knew, without a doubt, that he sounded exactly as he felt – jealous through to the marrow in his bones.

"If you must know," she replied, "I was talking to my dad and stepmom."

He was stupidly relieved and furious with himself. "I like your parents."

"They like you, too. Well," she said and grabbed an apple from the fruit bowl on the counter. "Goodnight."

David watched her leave, inhaled the familiar scent of her fragrance that always seemed to linger in the air and waited a few minutes before heading to his room. He checked on the kids, noticing that Scarlett was still restless and tossing in her bed. He grabbed the baby monitor he kept on hand for nights when the kids were poorly and walked into the master suite.

He kicked off his shoes and sat on the edge of the bed, setting up the monitor on the bedside table, in case he needed to get up in the middle of the night. The small framed photo of Jayne caught his attention. Loving her sometimes seemed like it happened in another lifetime.

A familiar ache pressed between his ribs and he looked at the wedding band on his left hand. He twirled the ring with his thumb and forefinger. It was looser than he remembered.

Memories seeped through him. And regrets. And grief. For so long he'd felt it hovering like a shadow. Afraid to remember. Afraid to forget. Wondering if he'd ever feel whole again.

David slipped the ring off, brought it to his lips for a moment, and then placed it in the drawer.

He wasn't sure why—but knew it was time.

Chapter Five

On Wednesday morning, Annie rounded up the kids, got them dressed and ready for the day, and then headed into town to take Jasper to school. He'd gotten passed the hugging stage about a year ago, preferring to high-five her at the school gate. But for the past couple of days, he'd clung to her, oblivious to his school friends walking past. Annie hugged him tightly, smoothing her hand over his hair, telling him she loved him.

"I saved my allowance," he said as she was crouched down in front of him, straightening his backpack. "You can have it if you want."

Annie looked at his serious expression. "Why would you want to give me your allowance...?" Her words trailed off and he shrugged in a way that was so much like David that her heart rolled over.

"I know Dad said it wasn't about money, but you know my friend Simon—well, his mom has a job at the library and she stayed there when she got more money—"

Annie squeezed his small shoulders gently, pain and guilt radiating through her entire body. "I don't look after you and Scarlett because of money," she assured him. "I do it because I love you both, very much. And just because I'm leaving, it doesn't mean I'll stop loving you both, or that you've done anything wrong."

He didn't look convinced or reassured and her heart ached, watching him enter the building, waving to him with Scarlett before heading back to the car.

She drove into town, listening to Scarlett chatting in the back. The youngest McCall attended nursery school, but David had elected to keep her home for the day, since she'd had a few restless nights, waking up several times and calling out.

Annie knew why. Both kids were naturally upset by her leaving, but while Jasper had gone quiet and brooding, Scarlett's emotions weren't as easily hidden.

Annie had a sketching class at the art gallery that morning and set Scarlett up beside her with paper and crayons. Once the class was done, she didn't linger with her classmates as she might normally do. They headed to the bakery for coffee, a mini milkshake for Scarlett and some pastries. Then they walked to David's office so that Scarlett could show off her artistic masterpiece to her father.

David's assistant, Kendra, was sitting at her desk in reception and greeted them warmly. David's door was open, but he was on a call, so Kendra asked them to wait with her. Scarlett raced around the desk to proudly show her art piece. Annie gave Kendra one of the take-out coffees and they chatted for a few minutes before David hung up the phone and called them into his office.

He was at the door when they entered and Scarlett rushed toward him, waving her painting.

"Daddy, look what I did!"

He hauled his daughter into his arms, looking incredibly sexy in a dark gray trousers, pale gray shirt and blue-patterned tie. She'd given him the tie for Christmas the year before and the gift had become something of a long-running joke between them, as she'd bought him one every Christmas since she'd been at the ranch. The first year had been a no-brainer, because she'd only been working for him for a few months and didn't know him well enough to give him anything more significant. But as one year merged into another, she did get to know him, and selected gifts that were meaningful and more personal…but she always added a tie, the funnier, the better. The one he now wore had flying blue elephants on it and always made her smile.

He looked up and met her gaze. "Hey, you look nice."

She glanced down at her green floral dress, cowboy boots and denim jacket. It was one of her favorite outfits. "Thank you." She passed him the take-out coffee and he took a sip. "We thought we'd stop by for a visit. I hope we're not interrupting?"

He quickly shook his head. "Of course not."

"Daddy," Scarlett said and kissed his cheek. "Guess what's in the bag?"

He glanced at the brown paper bag in Annie's hand. "I'm thinking my favorite bagel?"

"Nope," Scarlett said and giggled. "It's smaller." She made a tiny circle with her fingers.

David made a show of thinking extra hard. "Hmm... My favorite brownie?"

She giggled again. "No, Daddy! Keep guessing."

Annie's heart rolled over at the affection between the two of them. Scarlett was such a delightful child and so easy to love.

Annie listened as David kept guessing and then Scarlett laughed delightedly. "It's a cupcake!" she announced.

"My other favorite," he said and held his hand out for the bag.

Annie passed it to him and as their fingers touched; a shot of awareness raced up her arm. He jerked back, too, as though he'd been stung.

Could he be as affected as she was?

No. Impossible. It was crazy to even think it. She

couldn't count the number of times they'd accidently touched over the years, and even though she'd always experienced a jolt of electricity, David had never appeared to register the event on his radar.

But this was different. And he looked as surprised as she felt.

He shook his shoulders and stepped back, allowing Scarlett to open the bag. "Looks good," he said and lowered Scarlett to the floor. "Thank you, ladies," he said and grinned.

Scarlett took to his desk and jumped up in his seat to play "office," as she often did. "I'll take her home after this visit and see if I can get her down for a nap. She hasn't had nearly enough sleep this week."

"She's not the only one," he said pointedly and then sighed. "But she looks happier than she did last night."

Annie agreed, as she'd gotten up twice during the night to comfort Scarlett during her restless dreams. So had David.

"Jasper offered me his allowance," she said and quietly explained about the conversation. "He's taking it so hard."

"Naturally," David said. "He adores you. They both do."

Annie looked at him, her gaze honing in, and then noticing something different about his left hand. "You're not wearing your wedding ring?"

He glanced. "No, I'm not," he said and shrugged a little.

Her heart stupidly raced. "Why...now? I mean, after so long?"

"I think I kept it on so I could feel...normal," he said and shrugged again. "I don't know—like it would all seem too real without it. Stupid, I guess. Jayne's been gone for over four years. Some days it feels like an eternity and others, like it was yesterday."

"That's normal, I imagine, when you suffer such a significant loss."

He nodded. "Maybe. She would have liked you, you know. She'd approve of the way you put me in my place."

Annie grinned. "Did you need putting in your place back then?"

"Actually," he said quietly, "Jayne and I rarely had any disagreements. Arguing wasn't her style."

"Sounds like the perfect match."

"Perfect?" His gave a cynical grin. "Is there such a thing? Is that what you imagine you'll have with your fireman?"

Something about his tone made her lips quirk with a bit of a smile. "I don't know. He seems nice. Time will tell, I suppose."

"You should invite him here," he suggested. "To assess him on your own turf. Do a list of pros and cons."

Annie's eyes widened. "Hey, maybe I should do a flow chart, too," she remarked and shot one arched brow up. "And rate his attributes from one to ten."

"It's not a bad idea," he replied, suddenly scowling, the wrinkle between his brows deepening. "At least you'd know what you're getting into."

Annie laughed and waved her arm around the room. "You spend way too much time in here, David, with your numbers and spreadsheets. You've actually started believing that people are like some mathematic equation."

Her cell phone pinged with a text. She quickly checked the message and smiled.

"The boyfriend?"

She raised a brow. "Nope. My sister."

He looked…relieved.

Don't be foolish… Why would he really care?

"By the way," he said. "I heard back from the employment agency and have two interviews lined up for tomorrow. I thought I'd do them at the house, you know, to get a better sense of the *right fit*. I'd appreciate it if you would sit in on the interviews, just so I can get a second opinion."

Annie really didn't want to be a part of the hiring process, but she understood his motives. "Sure. I have to say, you've become very accepting of my decision all of a sudden."

He moved a little closer, out of earshot of Scarlett. "Would there be any point in my trying to convince you to stay?"

She shook her head, noticing how dark his green eyes looked. "No."

His gaze had never seemed more intense. "I'll

pick Jasper up from school," he said. "To save you another trip into town. And since I have a client arriving in about ten minutes, I really should get back to work."

Annie ignored the fluttering in her belly and quickly collected Scarlett. Once they were back in her car and on the way home, she relaxed fractionally, and thought about why David had suddenly decided to take off his wedding ring. And about why he was being so cordial and accepting of her departure all of a sudden. And why every time any mention of Byron came up in conversation, he acted a lot like he was...well...jealous.

Don't be absurd.

He's just mad because you're leaving and thinks Byron is to blame.

When she arrived back at the ranch, Annie immediately put Scarlett down for a nap, then headed to her own room, where she spent the next hour or so thinking about starting to sort and pack her clothes and then decided she didn't have the energy. So she puttered around the house, putting away some of the kids' toys until Scarlett woke from her nap.

David arrived home with Jasper just after four o'clock and she quickly took over, settling the boy with his reading homework, and then once he was done, she took both kids to the stables to check on the kittens.

Dinner was odd—almost strained. Mittie had gone into town for a canasta game with friends, and it was only the four of them, eating the chicken casserole Annie had whipped up that morning. Scarlett was clingy, hanging by her side for most of the meal. Jasper was quiet, David even quieter. When they were finished, she got the kids into their bath, changed into pajamas and settled in front of the television for a while before bedtime.

When she returned to the kitchen she found David loading the dishwasher, a frown marring his handsome face.

"Headache back?" she asked.

He looked up. "No. Just thinking."

In jeans and a T-shirt, he looked wholly masculine, and Annie's belly did its usual dive. "I can finish up here if you like?"

He shook his head. "It's fine. I was thinking you could take the night off. I promised Jasper I'd play a video game with him before bedtime. I'll get Scarlett settled once I'm done here."

Irrationally, Annie experienced an acute sense of *exclusion*. Which was stupid, because David *was* their father and he got the final say. "Okay, sure. I've got things to do anyway."

"Texting the fireman?"

And there it was. The snarky tone that seemed to have become the theme whenever Byron came up in conversation. "Maybe."

"Enjoy your evening," he said flatly as he closed the dishwasher and then strode from the room without another word.

* * *

"You know, David's being more unbearable than usual at the moment," Leah said.

Annie didn't disagree.

It was after ten the following morning and she was in the kitchen with Leah and Mittie, chatting about the older woman's upcoming Alaskan tour. Leah was several years younger than her brother and a talented artist, as well. She was also much more naturally outgoing than he was—easier to warm up to, which was why Annie had befriended her so quickly when they met.

Annie shrugged and took the coffee cup Mittie passed her and replied to Leah. "I guess he's got things on his mind."

"He's got *you* on his mind," Mittie announced, grinning broadly.

Annie almost spluttered her coffee across the table. "What?"

"Nan," Leah said and sighed. "Stop making things worse."

Annie looked at Leah and smiled. "Your grandmother is only—"

"Stirring," Leah said and raised both her brows. "We all know what David is like."

"Don't we just," Mittie said and chuckled. "I love my grandson, but he's one of those men who are never comfortable talking about their feelings. Even when Jayne and Sandra died, he closed down a lot. For a while I was concerned he'd never get over it.

But I think he has, even if he's not ready to admit it. I don't know why he doesn't just beg you to stay."

Beg? Annie laughed out loud. "I can't see that happening, can you? And anyway, it wouldn't make any difference."

"Because of Byron?" Leah queried.

Both women now knew about her online friendship with Byron. "Because," she said, choosing her words carefully, "it's time I moved on."

Mittie disappeared into the pantry and Leah spoke again.

"My brother's an idiot," she said and harrumphed.

Annie felt heat rise up her collarbone. "I don't know what you—"

"I know, Annie," Leah said gently. "I know why you're leaving."

The heat morphed into embarrassment and she sucked in a breath. How could she know? The only person who knew what was in her heart was her sister, and Tess would never betray her trust by saying anything. And heaven knew Annie had developed a tight lid on her feelings around the ranch. "I think you have the wrong idea. I just want to—"

Leah came around the countertop and gently squeezed her shoulder and as she regarded the woman, Annie experienced an unwavering sense of understanding. Of kinship. Of sisterhood. But she wouldn't show it. She couldn't. It was too humiliating.

"Annie?"

David's deep voice had them turning their gazes to the doorway. She wondered what he'd heard and then quickly got to her feet.

"Our first appointment is here."

With a steady glance toward Leah, Annie left the kitchen and followed David into his large office. A woman who looked to be in her midforties, with hair pulled back tightly from her face and wearing a neat black pantsuit, was already seated. Annie shook her hand as David introduced them.

Five minutes later, Annie knew she'd never allow the woman to watch over the kids. She was cold and uncompromising, mentioned nothing about having any affection for or continuing contact with her previous charges and was clearly a strict disciplinarian. The interview lasted about twenty minutes and Annie was just about prepared to stand up and tell the woman to get out when David ended the meeting and escorted the applicant to the front door, saying he'd get back to her by the end of the week. Once he returned to the office, Annie was standing by the window, arms crossed.

"So, what did you think?" he asked and moved around the desk.

Annie stared at him. "Of that woman? Very little."

His gaze narrowed. "That's pretty harsh."

"She is completely unsuitable."

"Really?" His brows came up as he sat down in his chair, swiveled around and faced her. "Why?"

She expelled a heavy breath. "She was…she was…cold. And unfeeling."

"Well, maybe that's for the best. Maybe I'd be wiser to find someone the kids won't get too attached to, so they don't suffer so much when the person leaves."

It was a direct dig and they both knew it. She didn't respond. Didn't say a word.

He looked at her, then laughed. "The truth hard to handle, Annie?"

She ignored that he was laughing at her. "Look, they're your kids and you can make any decision you want, but you asked me for my opinion and I'm giving it. That woman will make your life a living hell."

David's mouth turned up slightly. "Unlike you, you mean?" he quipped as he shuffled a few papers on his desk.

"Oh, so you want someone who says yes to everything?"

"I want someone who'll stay," he replied tightly.

It was a low blow, designed to make her feel bad—which it did. He was so wrapped up in his own world he really had no clue what it was doing to her. "See you later," she said and turned to leave the room.

"Hang around," he said quickly. "Our next appointment will be here in a few minutes."

"I'll come back."

"Or wait," he said and looked up, motioning to one of the seats opposite. "And we could talk."

Her suspicions rose. "About what?"

"The kids, of course." He met her gaze head-on. "We both know they are struggling at the moment. Jasper's closing off and Scarlett isn't sleeping at night. I'm worried about my kids, Annie."

Her insides crunched up. "I know that. So am I."

"But not enough to reconsider, right?"

"Did you really think I'd stay forever?" she asked quickly.

He got to his feet in a microsecond. "I don't know," he said with a sigh. "The truth is, I didn't *think*. Things have been a certain way around here for so long I just got used to it."

"I became invisible, you mean?" she asked sharply.

"That's not what I mean," he said, clearly exasperated.

Well, he wasn't the only one.

"I'm not sure what changed for you," he said, continuing the conversation. "But for some reason whenever I ask why you're leaving, you make me feel as though I have done something wrong, and all I want to do is fix it."

Annie held on to her resolve. She wouldn't fall apart. Wouldn't crumble. Wouldn't let him see how much she was hurting.

"You can't fix it," she replied, adrenaline seeping through her veins. "I know you want things to stay the same, because this," she said and waved an arm in an arc, "the way things are, is easy for you. You have it all under control. All your ducks in a row. However, I want a different life. And if you can't see that," she said, her voice rising with each word, "then you're selfish as well as blind."

His gaze narrowed. "If your opinion of me is so low, I'm surprised you've hung around for the last four years. Frankly, I can't believe you didn't bail ages ago."

"Maybe I should have," she said hotly, humiliation scorching her cheeks. "At least that way I wouldn't love—" She stopped abruptly, realizing she was a word away from completely embarrassing herself.

"You wouldn't love?"

"The kids," she replied, her skin burning when she saw the way his brows rose up as he looked at her. "I wouldn't love the kids as much as I do."

"And yet," he reminded her. "You're still leaving them. You're leaving *us*!"

"And the fact you continue to—"

"Ah, guys," a voice said from the doorway. "Your next appointment is here."

They both turned and spotted Leah standing there. David spoke quickly. "Of course, I'll see her in."

"And would you guys stop arguing," Leah said and shook her head. "We could hear you from the kitchen."

Annie crossed her arms. "Sorry."

"What's going on with you two?" Leah said and

frowned. "It's like you can't even bear to be in the same room as each other."

"We weren't arguing," David said quietly. "And even if we were, it wouldn't be anyone's business," he said as he headed from the room.

Leah made a face in Annie's direction. "Phew, Annie, please reconsider leaving—I'm afraid my brother is going to go loco the day you walk out."

"He'll get over it," she said and shrugged. "And for the record, he was right, we weren't arguing, we were simply having a discussion."

Leah grinned. "Yeah…sure you were. I have to get going, but call me if you need to talk," she said and then added, "about anything."

Once Leah was gone, Annie lingered by the window, looking outside to where David had already greeted the next applicant. This one was young. Very young. And perky. And blond. With legs encased in leggings that seemed to go on forever.

Okay, nothing wrong with leggings. Plenty of women wore them. She wore them all the time!

Although, perhaps not for a job interview with a sexy single dad.

Her name, Annie discovered a couple of minutes later once they were all seated in the office, was Becca. She was twenty years old and had recently finished studying fashion design at the technical college in Rapid City. She loved kids, of course, and would like nothing more than to look after the children, since she'd had so much experience baby-sitting during her high school years.

"I exercise every day, and I could take the kids on power walks, so we'd have a lot of fun together," the younger woman said. "And it would be a healthy activity," she added with so much exuberance that Annie rolled her eyes and then glanced toward David, immediately noticing that he was watching her. She turned her gaze to the floor, ignoring the heat in her own cheeks and the tiny smile on his mouth. Because he clearly knew she was unimpressed with Becca's credentials. Or lack thereof!

By the time the post-teen was finished talking about herself, another ten minutes had passed. Once David escorted her out, promising to be in touch, Annie stalked around the room, arms crossed, irritation rising with every breath she took. By the time he returned, she was rolling her eyes.

"Seriously?" she said to him before he'd barely entered the room.

"What?" he said.

"They were the best candidates?"

"Of the recommendations I could get on short notice? I thought so."

She frowned. "Then you need to broaden your search. Maybe even look farther than this town."

"Sure," he said easily.

Too easily.

"Are you saying that simply to get me off your back?"

One brow rose and his mouth curled at the corners. "I didn't realize you were *on* my back."

The innuendo hung in the air between them and she colored hotly. "What's gotten into you?"

"I could ask you the same thing. Although I think we both know this sudden infatuation with the fireman is the real reason you are —"

"Do you want to know the *real* reason?" she asked hotly, cutting him off. "And it's one that hasn't got anything to do with me wanting my own life, or Byron, or anything else."

His gaze locked with hers. "Please…enlighten me."

Annie pushed back her shoulders and expelled a long breath. "It's because it's just too hard to be around you anymore!"

She stalked past him and left the room, her chest so tight her ribs ached. She raced down the hall and headed for her rooms, slammed the door and flopped onto the couch, every part of her hurting.

She was on the verge of letting the tears flow when there was a sharp rap on her door. She got to her feet, rubbed her hand over her face and walked across the room, only to find David standing on the other side of the door.

Annie sucked in a breath and stared at him.

"What do you want?" If she sounded rude, she didn't care. But she wasn't in the mood for an argument or a rehash of the very obvious tension burning between them.

"To talk." He said and then sighed. "To apologize."

Annie turned on her heel and walked further into the room. She stood by the couch and faced him, hands on her hips.

"So, talk."

"I'm sorry, okay?" he said quietly and moved across the room, standing a few feet from her. "I shouldn't have made that remark about your personal life. And I shouldn't have—"

"Set up two interviews with people clearly unfit for the role of looking after your children because you wanted to make me feel guilty for leaving?" Annie was so mad and *so* hurt, her chest heaved. "Does that about cover it?"

He took a breath, nodding a little. "Like I said, I'm sorry."

Annie glared at him, noticing that he looked tired, as though he hadn't slept much. She shouldn't have cared that he was probably having sleepless nights thinking about who would watch over his children once she was gone, but she did. "Stop making this hard for me."

"I can't," he admitted.

"Why?" she asked, surprised by his candor.

"Because I don't want you to go."

"Why, David? Because I make your life easier?" she reminded him.

He shook his head, and she could see the conflicting emotion in his expression and realized, maybe for the first time, that there was more to this than his need for an orderly life. "It doesn't feel easy at the moment. It feels like…."

She suddenly became aware that he was in front of her, his chest heaving, staring at her in a way that put every sense she possessed on red alert. Somehow, something had changed in their relationship over the previous days and the man standing in front of her—watching her with such burning intensity— was not the David she was used to. A pulse throbbed in his cheek, his eyes were dark and he looked completely out of sorts, as though he was searching for what to say, what to do. He looked as though he was hanging on by a thread.

She smiled, foolishly trying to make things easier for him. Her heart hammered so loud she was certain he could hear it. Certain he'd know what she was feeling, that he could see the longing in her eyes. For four years she'd hidden it, determined he would never know the truth—that she wanted him so much. Because he didn't want her that way. He never looked at her with desire.

Until now.

"It feels like…what?" she whispered, her heart pounding, her legs weakening.

And then, just as in her secret dreams, his hand reached out and he gently cupped her nape, drawing her close.

"It feels like I am out of control," he said, his voice raw.

So was she, in that moment. The searing heat from his fingertips warmed her entire body. Of course, they had been physically close many times—like when he was teaching her to ride a horse, or when they were helping the children with their homework or a new project or even when they were up late washing dishes in the kitchen, which they often did together.

But this was different. This was pure and unadulterated intimacy. The kind she'd never expected to experience with him.

"Annie..."

He said her name so softly, almost as though he was saying it against his will and she swallowed hard, noticing everything about him in that moment—the way his green eyes had suddenly darkened, the tiny scar on his left temple, the way his mouth curled up a little.

He grasped her chin gently, tilted her head upward and gazed at her with such heat her insides quivered as she realized, without a shred of doubt, that he was going to kiss her.

This is so crazy...

David said the words to himself over and over, repeating them like a chant from the moment he'd crossed the threshold into Annie's room. Her domain. Her world. A place he didn't belong. How could he? She worked for him and it was his responsibility to maintain the professionalism between them. But he hadn't expected to feel so inexplicably drawn to her. He hadn't expected the building awareness and attraction he had for her to take hold so hard.

He hadn't expected to suddenly want to kiss her so badly.

Not suddenly. That was a lie. All week it had messed with his good sense, making him think about her when he should have been doing a dozen other things. And now, as he felt her lips touch his, David was at the mercy of the reckless attraction that he'd fought so hard to ignore.

She sighed, then pressed her lips against his and David instinctively moved closer, deepening the kiss. Her mouth opened and he let her take the lead. Her tongue moved between their lips, winding around his, awakening feelings he'd suppressed for a long time—forever, he'd thought. Until now. Every shred of defense he'd put up over the years, every sermon he'd silently preached to himself about boundaries, suddenly and spectacularly disappeared. Her mouth, her breath, the sweet sensation of her tongue against his own—nothing had prepared him for the rush of desire it created and the way his body reacted.

David prided himself on always being in control, but beneath the softness of Annie's mouth, every inch of his control slipped away, and he was completely at her mercy. Instinct tormented him and he fought against the need to press closer, to feel her lovely curves against him, to plunge his tongue deeper into her mouth.

Holy freaking hell!

David wrenched himself free, breathing so hard he thought he might pass out. She looked no better as she took a couple of steps backward and stared at him, her chest rising and falling so rapidly he had to pull on every ounce of self-control he had left to not look at it. He wasn't that guy. He'd *never* been that guy. He respected women. He respected Annie. And he had too much self-respect to overstep acceptable boundaries.

"Annie." He said her name, hating the way he sounded like he couldn't quite get enough air into his lungs. "I'm really… I don't know what happened then… I'm so…"

"You kissed me," she said bluntly, trying to catch her breath. "I kissed you back. That's what happened."

Heat crawled up his neck. "I'm sorry, Annie, that was way out of bounds. I didn't come in here to—"

"Forget it," she said and waved a hand casually. But David wasn't fooled. She was as wound up by the events of the last sixty seconds as he was. "Let's just…let's just not overanalyze this. Okay?"

David's insides twitched. Yeah, he would forget it. That was the sensible thing to do. But he didn't believe she was so easily motivated to ignore the heat between them, or the fact that he'd practically kissed her senseless. "Okay. Uh…" He wasn't sure what to say, since she seemed to want him gone. "I'll talk to you later?"

"Sure," she said dismissively and walked toward the door. "Whatever."

David turned on his heel and followed, lingering by the door for a moment. "I meant what I said, Annie. What just happened was a mistake and I'm sorry."

He left and headed back to the main house, walked directly to his office, shut the door and sat at his desk for half an hour. He turned his laptop on and off twice, he pushed papers around his desk, he changed the ink cartridge in his fountain pen. He did anything and everything he could to take his mind off the problem at hand and after thirty minutes, gave up trying.

He found his grandmother in the kitchen, making cupcakes, and once he'd poured himself coffee, sat across the countertop.

"Something on your mind?" Mittie asked, one brow higher than the other.

David glanced at his grandmother and shrugged a little. "Nope."

"You always were a terrible liar."

He ignored her. "Where's Leah?"

"I'm not sure. Maybe with Annie."

He sipped his coffee. "Did she say anything to you?"

"Leah?

"No," he said irritably. "Annie."

"About what?" Mittie asked, icing the cupcakes.

"About anything?"

"No," his grandmother replied. "Should she have?"

He shrugged again. "Ah...no."

"I heard you arguing before," Mittie said and shook her head with disapproval. "Not helping the situation."

Nothing he did helped the situation. Particularly kissing Annie! But he wasn't about to say that to his grandmother. "It's complicated."

"What's complicated?"

It was his stepdad's voice he heard from the back door. Ivan shrugged out of his jacket and hung it on a peg by the door, then sat on the stool beside him.

"The Annie situation," Mittie explained and widened her eyes as she passed Ivan a coffee mug. "You know," she added and jerked her gaze in David's direction.

"Still intent on leaving, is she?"

Mittie nodded. "Looks that way."

"So," Ivan said and elbowed David in the ribs. "What are you going to do about it?"

"Do?" David echoed. "There's nothing I can do."

"Really? It's not like you to give in so easily."

"She's got it into her head that she wants to leave," he said quietly. "I can't make her change her mind."

"Of course you can," Ivan said and grinned. "Use your charm."

"I'm all out," he said humorlessly.

"You simply have to find out what she wants," his stepdad said and nodded. "Easy."

"I know what she wants," he said and grimaced as he drained his coffee mug. "She wants to get married and have a baby."

"Then marry her and give her a baby," Ivan said and grinned. "Before someone else does."

David pushed himself off the stool and got to his feet. He didn't want to hear it. Didn't want to think it. Didn't want to acknowledge, even for a second, that the idea of her marrying the fireman or anyone else, was eating away at him. "Don't be ridiculous."

"What's ridiculous about it?" Ivan shot back. "Unless you don't find her attractive?"

"No," he said quickly and then shook his head. "Of course she's… I mean, I don't think about her in that way."

Big fat lie number one.

"Because?" his stepdad asked.

"Because it would be inappropriate and I'm not going to have this conversation," he said impatiently.

"Inappropriate because she works for you?" Ivan inquired.

"Exactly."

His stepfather's eyes widened. "So when she's not working for you, in…" he paused and counted numbers on his fingers, "…a few weeks, it won't be inappropriate?"

David frowned. "Well…yes. But then the point will be moot because I'll hire another nanny and won't need her to—" He stopped speaking and shook his head. "Like I said, I'm not having this conversation."

"You mean the thought has never crossed your mind?" Ivan asked.

"Of course not."

Big fat lie number two...

Because it had. It was all he could think about. Dream about. And he was confused by his feelings.

He needed to get a grip. And fast.

He needed to stop thinking about Annie running off to marry some man she'd never met. A stranger who didn't know how beautiful she was, how caring, how important she was to everyone.

And mostly, how important she was to him.

Chapter Six

"Has David found your replacement yet?"

Annie smiled at her sister as she stretched out on the yoga mat. Tess has started attending the classes with her and she was delighted for the company. Hanging out with her sister was one of her favorite things to do. And Thursday night yoga class was their opportunity to talk and catch up. David usually finished work early on Thursdays and spent extra time with the children, which gave her a free evening.

"No," she replied and stretched out her calves. "He has another two interviews scheduled for tomorrow. Both applicants with the right references." She'd told her sister about the two unsuitable candidates they'd interviewed the day before. She hadn't told her about the argument or the kiss. Mostly because she couldn't believe it actually happened. Her lips still tingled at the memory. Her heart ached knowing he'd said it was a mistake. Which of course it was, and obviously it didn't mean anything. But Tess was a romantic and would read way more into it than it actually meant.

After the yoga class they lingered for twenty minutes at the gym café, chatting over a green smoothie. "Have you heard from Byron?" Tess asked and grinned.

She nodded. "Most days we trade a couple of texts."

"Have you made any firm plans to meet him?"

She shook her head a fraction. "I didn't want any more complications. You know…while I'm still living at the ranch."

"And once you're not living there?" Tess probed.

"Then there will be no reason why we can't meet up, see if there's something between us worth pursuing."

"Well, from what you've said, he seems very nice. And he obviously likes you," Tess added and grinned. "And you like him, right?"

"Of course," she replied.

"You should invite him here," her sister said as she finished her smoothie. "So we can check him out."

"That's what David said, too."

Tess raised a brow quizzically. "So, how are things between you two?"

Forever changed...

"Okay," she replied.

Tess nodded, but Annie knew her sister could see through her assurances. "By the way, how are you going with your speech for the christening?"

Happy for the change of subject, she smiled. "Good. I'm honored, you know, to be named Charlie's godparent," Annie said, a lump of emotion in her throat. "I know there are a lot of people you and Mitch could have named as—"

"Of course it's you," Tess said, cutting her off. "Well, you and David."

Annie jerked back in her seat. "David? I thought Jake would be—"

"David is Mitch's closest friend," Tess reminded her. "As well as his cousin. And we both trust David, like we trust you. There are no two people we would trust more to love our son."

Annie's eyes burned. "Thank you. And I promise I will always—"

"I know," Tess said and patted her arm. "I thought perhaps you'd like to stay at the Triple C for a while, once you leave your job."

She told her sister about how she'd booked a room at the O'Sullivan hotel for a few days. "I think the hotel will be better," she replied and smiled. "Once I make some firm plans about the future, I'll let you know."

"I hope you stay in Cedar River," Tess said, her eyes shining. "I love being able to see you so often. Living in Sioux Falls after I divorced Mitch was hard without you close by. Selfish, I know," Tess added. "But I feel like a better version of myself when we're in the same town. And I want my son to really know his aunt."

Annie hugged her sister. "I want that, too."

By the time Annie returned to the ranch it was past nine o'clock. She knew the kids would be asleep and Mittie usually turned in around eight thirty as she was an early riser. She spotted the office light on through the front window, and figuring David was working and the coast was clear, headed to the kitchen for a snack. David, however, wasn't in his office. He was sitting at the kitchen table with a small stack of documents in front of him, his legs stretched out, a coffee mug in one hand.

"Oh, hi," she said and moved around the countertop.

He looked up and his mouth crinkled at the edges. "Hey there. How was your class?"

Annie nodded. "Both exhausting and relaxing. What are you doing?" she asked, trying to sound casual, and trying not to think about how the mood between them had become increasingly awkward. And trying not to think about the kiss.

"Résumés," he replied and pushed one across the table. "For our interviews tomorrow. The one on top is for the woman who used to be a schoolteacher.

She's been looking after her grandchildren for the past three years while her daughter was deployed overseas. Now her daughter has finished her tour she's available to work a few days a week, dividing her time between her grandkids and a job."

Annie's back straightened. "You're thinking of getting someone part-time?"

He nodded. "For the time being. I don't want to commit to a full-time nanny at this stage. I know the kids need routine and stability, but this is a good opportunity for me to make a few changes."

Annie came toward the table. "What kind of changes?"

"Taking on another CPA, for starters," he said and straightened, pulling his legs beneath the table. "My client base has grown to the point where I need to look at sharing the load, which will give me more time at home." He met her gaze levelly. "The truth is, after Jayne and my mom died, I think I checked out for while, if that makes sense. You know…emotionally."

Annie nodded. "That's understandable, though. You were grieving."

"And then I had you to look after my kids," he said and sighed. "I'm very grateful for how quickly you picked up the pieces- for all of us."

Annie's insides contracted. "David, you're a great dad and the kids adore you." She hesitated, knowing how the mention of his late wife tended to affect him. "Jayne would be really proud of how well you take care of them."

"I'd like to think so. When the kids were younger it seemed easier somehow. Of course, some ways are harder, sleepless nights and diapers and teething. But now, they're little people and need a different kind of care. Scarlett was only a couple of months old when Jayne died, but the truth is, I was working all the time and Jayne was always happiest in the air." He smiled, as though lost in thought and memory for a moment. "I never really understood, I suppose. She had an adventurous spirit and a need to be free."

"I'm sure she knew you loved her." Annie quickly wished she could swallow the words back. She didn't need to think about how much David had adored his wife. And probably still did.

He nodded. "We met in college, we dated, we got engaged, we got married. It just sort of happened. We never questioned why we were together and we had a happy marriage. We didn't argue. We didn't make demands. I knew what was important to her and she knew what was important to me. I guess you could say we grew up together. Marriage is about compromise."

"I wouldn't know."

His eyes widened. "But you *do* want to get married, correct?"

Annie nodded, hoping he couldn't see the heavy flush rising up her neck. "Yes."

"And you think the fireman is the man for you?"

She shrugged. "I don't know. Maybe."

"Have you ever been in love?"

It was an impossibly personal question and she couldn't believe he was asking it. But there was no doubting the curiosity in his expression. Annie swallowed hard and took a short breath. "Once," she admitted.

"And what happened?"

She quickly caught the gasp in her throat. "He didn't love me back."

David's eyes darkened. "Stupid man."

"I've always thought so," she said and quickly moved around the counter and grabbed a glass, then poured some water. She drank a little before looking up and discovered David watching her intently. "What?"

He got to his feet and came to the countertop, resting his hands palms down on the bench. "We haven't really talked about what happened yesterday."

The heat in her cheeks intensified. "I'd rather not rehash it," she said, dying inside, not wanting to hear about how sorry he was for kissing her because he believed it was such a big mistake. She looked at the clock. "Well, it's late, and I've got to get the kids to school in the morning. Good night." She put her glass in the sink and turned to head for the back door.

"I was thinking we could take the kids out to JoJo's for pizza tomorrow night," he said, not moving. "I know they want to spend as much time with you as they can before…" He swallowed. "Well, before you go."

Annie didn't think it was a good idea. For a hundred reasons. But the idea of upsetting the children was impossible to bear, so she nodded. "Sure, sounds great."

He straightened. "Good night, Annie. Sleep well."

Annie turned and set off for her room as though her heels were on fire.

After two interviews the following morning, David decided to offer the position to the grandmother looking for a part-time job. He wanted someone trustworthy and reliable and since he knew his chances of finding someone as perfect as Annie were impossible, those qualities would need to be enough.

Someone as perfect as Annie…

Funny, but he'd only just come to realize how true that was. She'd accused him of treating her as though she was invisible. He'd denied it at the time, but since then he'd had days to think about, and now he realized she might be right.

He'd taken her for granted and now he was paying the price. She was on the verge of leaving and would soon have a different life. With someone else. With the fireman. She'd fall in love with him. Marry him. Have children with him.

And he couldn't bear thinking about it.

"She was nice," Annie said when he returned to the office after the last interview. "You were right."

"Sometimes that has been known to happen," he said and grinned a little when he saw she was smiling. "Doesn't look like I'm going to be getting back to town today."

"Two days this week working from home," she said. "That must be a record."

"Am I that much of a workaholic?"

She nodded. "Sometimes."

She was still smiling and looked so pretty that David had to remind himself to not stare at her like an infatuated teenager. She wore a short denim dress, ballet flats and her hair was up in a loose ponytail. She had nice legs—smooth and athletic—no doubt from the yoga and running and horse riding. In fact, everything about her was breathtakingly sexy. He liked her curves and the way she moved was incredibly alluring.

"David?"

Her voice jerked him from his foolish trance and he met her gaze "Yes?"

"Everything okay?"

"Perfect," he said and smiled. "I thought we'd head into town around six. Does that work?"

"Sure," she said and , watching him curiously for a moment before she turned and left the room.

He spent the next hour checking references for the woman he planned on hiring, and when they came back without a hitch, he called her and offered her the position. She accepted immediately and David worked out a start date. He finished up in the office around four. The kids were home from school by then so he spent some time with them before Annie got them bathed and dressed.

He showered, changed into jeans, a black button-down shirt and boots and then headed back to the kitchen just before six o'clock. His grandmother was making tea and the kids were seated at the table, dressed and ready to go.

Mittie looked up and grinned. "Big date?"

David frowned. "Don't start. You're welcome to come with us."

His grandmother shook her head. "I have a busy weekend planned. I'm playing in the mah-jongg tournament at the veterans' home tomorrow, so I'll be needing an extra early night."

David was about to respond when Annie appeared in the doorway and his jaw almost dropped to his feet. She wore a pale blue dress, knee length and buttoned at the front, and a pair of sparkly orange-and-blue cowboy boots. Her hair was loose, tumbling down her back and the dress highlighted every lovely curve. David caught the appreciative sigh from his lips before he gave it sound and he swallowed hard.

"Ready?" he asked, ignoring the twitch in his limbs.

She nodded, avoiding his gaze. "Let's go, kids."

The children were out of their seats in a microsecond and a couple of minutes later were buckled in the rear of his SUV.

"You look really nice," he said as he started the ignition.

She took a moment to respond. "Thank you."

Once they were on the road and driving into town, he spoke again. "Is there somewhere you'd like me to send your things?" he asked evenly. "I know you have several pieces of your own furniture in your room."

"Tess said she'd store them at the Triple C until I get settled," she replied.

David shrugged. "I guess you could, but I can't see the point hiring anyone to move your stuff for such a short time. You may as well leave them here. The new nanny won't be a live-in. No point in moving the stuff twice. I mean, if you decide to go to Texas, you can just get it moved directly there."

She didn't respond and David turned his gaze toward her briefly, hoping she'd contradict his comment. But she didn't.

"Or not," he added.

"I think I'll just replace it when I figure out my next steps. You can take it down to the cabin, if you want. You said the place needed a few things to make it more livable."

"So," he continued. "So where will you go once you leave? To stay with Tess at the Triple C?"

"No, I'm going to stay at O'Sullivan's for a few

days," she replied. "Just to get my bearings. After that I haven't made any firm decisions."

David was pleased to hear it. At least she wasn't racing off to Texas immediately. "Do you plan on working somewhere?"

"Of course," she replied. "I thought I'd try to get a position back in office admin. I have a couple of applications to send out."

"If you need references, let me know."

"Oh, I will," she said. "I must say, you've become very agreeable all of a sudden."

"It's not sudden," he replied. "I've simply realized that trying to talk you out of leaving is futile."

"What does *futile* mean, Daddy?"

Jasper's quiet voice cut through their conversation. David glanced at his son in the rearview mirror. "It means there's no point."

"Like when I don't want to eat brussels sprouts?"

David grinned. "Something like that."

"Or peas!" Scarlett said, chiming in.

"You love peas," Annie reminded his daughter.

Scarlett giggled. "I forgot. Daddy, will our new mommy make Jasper eat brussels sprouts?"

David sucked in a breath. *New mommy?* Of course…because in many ways Scarlett regarded Annie as her mother. And probably Jasper did, too.

"Say something to them," she whispered in a stern tone, glaring at him.

David cleared his throat and spoke. "Kids, you know that even though a nanny takes you to school, and tucks you in at night and reads you a bedtime story, she's not your mommy, right?"

Scarlett looked puzzled, and her lip began to tremble. David looked at his daughter in the rearview mirror and his heart dropped. "Someday, you'll have a mommy again, honey," he said, desperate to comfort his children.

"They will?" Annie asked, her voice so low he knew the kids couldn't hear her.

He shrugged and turned off toward town. "Sure."

"You know, that means you'd have to get married again?"

"I know what it means," he replied quietly. "I'm not antimarriage. I liked being married. In fact, I think I was pretty good at it."

She made a slight huffing sound. "I didn't realize you were open to such a commitment."

"I wasn't," he said and jerked his gaze sideways for a second, getting a clear view of her tightly wired jaw and unblinking eyes. "But who knows what the future might hold?"

The last thing Annie wanted to do was think about David getting married.

Second last, she corrected. The very last thing she wanted to do was spend an hour or so at JoJo's pizza parlor and pretend that she wasn't dying inside.

Of course the kids quickly pulled her out of her funk and once they were seated and had ordered, she listened as Jasper spoke about the latest book on dragons that he was reading. Jasper usually didn't say much—he was like his father in that way—but she'd sensed his need for quiet conversation and reassurance for days. And Scarlett clung to her, holding her hand, demanding hugs and kisses before bedtime. Determined to make the transition as easy as possible for the children, Annie realized she needed to lots of time with both of them over the ensuing weeks, so they both understood why she was leaving in a way that made them feel safe and loved.

As she watched the kids munching on breadsticks, Annie's logic blurred. She'd always known how hard leaving them would be, but faced with the reality that her departure from their lives was only a couple of weeks away, an ache formed deep within her chest. She loved them, and knew the feelings were reciprocated and suddenly experienced an acute sense of loss that rocked her to the core.

"Are you okay, Annie?"

David's deep voice pulled her from her thoughts. "I'm fine."

"You look pale."

"Must be the lighting in here," she said and grabbed a breadstick. "Or just my complexion."

He rested his elbows on the table and linked his hands. "You have nice skin."

Annie's cheeks burned. She wasn't used to compliments from him. "That's sweet to say."

"Sweet?" he mused and grinned slightly. "Don't think I've ever been called that before."

Annie tried to bite back the smile forming on her lips and failed. "I'm sure Mittie thinks so."

David chuckled. "As my grandmother, she's biased."

Annie suspected Mittie thought her grandson hung the moon. "She is, but everyone else can't be wrong."

He laughed again and the deep, sexy sound made her skin goose bump. "To know me is to love me, you mean?"

Emotion rose through her blood, but she still managed a shaky smile. "I wouldn't... I wouldn't go that far."

His gaze darkened. "Annie, after all this time you know me pretty well."

"I guess I do."

Their pizza arrived before he could respond and Annie spent the following minutes dishing out slices to the kids and peeling the crust off Scarlett's piece. David chatted to Jasper about a new video game he wanted for his birthday the following month, while she tended to Scarlett and she figured that to an on-looker, they would appear to be a run-of-the-mill family. The moment became all the more poignant to Annie when she realized it might be the last time they would be out together as a group. The notion deeply saddened her and she shuddered.

"Everything all right?" David asked, swaying a little closer to her.

She nodded. "Sure. Fine."

Of course it wasn't the truth, but she couldn't let him know that. The remainder of dinner was done quickly. The kids pleaded for gelato, and they devoured it with giggles and messy hands. Annie cleaned them up before they headed home and they both fell asleep in the backseat well before the vehicle hit the highway. When they arrived at the ranch, David carried Jasper inside to his room and Annie did the same with Scarlett. She was changing the dozing child into her pajamas when she spotted David coming through the doorway of the bedroom.

"Jasper didn't stir," he whispered and flicked on the night-light. "Kid could sleep through a tornado."

Annie smiled, tucked the blanket around Scarlett's shoulders and the youngster stirred and moaned. "Not this one," she said softly and gently placed Scarlett's favorite teddy alongside her pillow. "She's too busy being a part of the world."

He looked down at his now sleeping child. "She really is amazing. So full of life. She'll never be tied down...like her mom, I guess."

Annie heard the melancholy in his voice and her gaze strayed to the small, framed photograph of Jayne McCall on the bedside table. "Roots and wings."

He nodded. "You mean, she's got a predictable stick-in-the-mud like me for a father and her mom was the free spirit? You're right. Although Jayne did have a pragmatic side to her."

"I don't think you're a stick-in-the-mud," she said

as they headed from the room and walked down the hallway.

He grinned. "Thanks, but I'm an accountant... I'm supposed to be a bore."

"You're not boring," she said, way too quickly as they rounded the corner and entered the kitchen. "You're...you're..."

"I'm?" he prompted. "What?"

Annie blinked a couple of times, adjusting her eyes to the brighter light in the room. "You're... you know...*you*."

He laughed. "I'm not sure that's a compliment."

"It is," she said and shrugged. "Well, I think I'll turn in. Thank you for dinner."

"Annie," he said and reached out, grabbing her hand.

She felt the warmth of his touch right down to the soles of her feet. "What?"

He didn't move. "I know tonight was hard for you. I mean, I know you're going to miss them," he said quietly, right on point. "They'll miss you, too. And so will I," he added.

In her heart, she knew he would...but not for the reasons she wanted...or needed.

"You'll get into another routine with someone else," she said, thinking she should move and put space between them, thinking she should pull away and not like the touch of his hand so much, but she didn't. "And life will go on, as normal."

His gaze stayed with hers. "Is that what you think

you are to me, Annie? Merely routine? I assure you, that's not the case."

"Then what—"

"Annie," he said, his voice sharp, almost breathless as he cut her off. "Marry me?"

Chapter Seven

"*What* did you say?"

Annie stepped back and pulled her hand free, staring at him, thinking she must have misheard... or that he had suddenly lost his mind.

"Marry me," he said again.

It was official...he was insane.

"That's the craziest thing I've ever—"

"It's not crazy," he said quickly, cutting off her protest. "Think about it... It makes perfect sense. The kids—"

"It's not about the kids," she said, mortified by the mixture of feelings surging through her blood... like disbelief and shock and something else...something she wasn't prepared to admit.

"They love you," he said flatly. "And they need you."

"*They* love me," she shot back. "Exactly. But *you* don't," she said and couldn't bear how much saying the words hurt her. "And I don't—"

"I know that we don't care about one another in that way, Annie," he said and sighed heavily. "But sometimes, marriages start out for different reasons. Who's to say what's the right way. And we can't predict how we'll feel in the future, can we? You said you were leaving because you wanted to get married...so, let's get married."

Annie couldn't believe what she was hearing. Never, in all her wildest dreams, did she imagine David would resort to a marriage proposal to keep her looking after his children. The fact he believed her so desperate to get married that she would actually consider it, hurt her bone deep. Like he was prepared to make himself a human sacrifice.

"You'd actually marry me to stop me from leaving?" she asked incredulously and crossed her arms.

"Yes..." He shook his head. "No... I mean. It wouldn't be like that...so cut and dried. I care about you, Annie. And I thought..." He paused, looking at her with searing intensity. "Is this about the fireman?" he asked, his expression narrowing.

"What?"

"Your online boyfriend," he reminded her. "Is your reaction because of him?"

Annie inhaled, sucking air into her lungs. "My reaction, as you call it, has nothing to do with Byron," she replied hotly. "It's about how I value myself too much to consider a loveless marriage with someone who is asking because it's convenient."

"That's not why," he returned quickly. "I just thought—"

"Save it," she said and waved a hand impatiently. "Come on, David... you've probably worked it out in your head that this arrangement would fix your problem of hiring a new nanny. I imagine you've probably done one of your famous pro-and-con lists and come out thinking that marrying me would make your life a whole lot easier. Well, all it would do is complicate the hell out of mine! Did you ever think about *that*?"

She shoved past him and headed down the hall, racing to her room. Annie dropped onto the sofa and pressed a hand to her chest, trying to get her heart rate back to normal.

Marry me...

David's words echoed around in her head. How could he resort to such a tactic?

A loveless marriage...

And she couldn't do it. She *wouldn't* do it. Not even if, for the tiniest of moments, she could envision that it wouldn't be loveless. That he had somehow discovered that he couldn't live without her for reasons of his own—and not only because he wanted a mother for his kids.

Because he *had* to know what his proposal would

do to her. He wasn't that self-absorbed—was he? He knew she loved Jasper and Scarlett with all her heart and wouldn't put them in that kind of situation.

With a sigh, Annie walked into her bedroom, stripping off her clothes. He'd said she looked nice in her outfit. Was it a line? A compliment to make her think he actually noticed her as more than an employee? As a woman? And potentially, as his wife?

She flopped on the bed and stared at the ceiling, fatigue seeping through her bones. But how could she sleep? Her mind was churning.

Her heart was aching.

Surprisingly, Annie did sleep and dragged herself out of bed early the following morning feeling groggy and completely drained. It was her day off, so she slipped into jeans, boots and a light sweater, skipped her usual coffee fix and headed to the Triple C, managing to avoid being seen by anyone in the house. When she pulled up at the Culhane ranch twenty minutes later she spotted Mitch in the main corral, guiding a beautiful-looking colt on a lead rein. Annie rested a toe on the fence post and watched for a moment.

"Hey there, Annie," Mitch said when he noticed her.

Annie smiled. "Hi. Is this one of the Alvarez foals?" she asked and climbed up one rung on the fence to get a better look at the colt.

"Sure is. This is Monty."

Annie knew a little about the new breeding program at the Triple C and how Mitch had gone into business with Ramon Alvarez, a horseman from Arizona. From all accounts it was the first time the other man had struck a deal outside his home state and she was told the new bloodline from Alvarez's champion stallion would help maintain Mitch's reputation as one of the best horse trainers and breeders in South Dakota.

"He's beautiful."

"Tess is nursing Charlie," he said and led the colt toward the fence.

"Actually, I was looking for you. I was wondering if I could leave Star here for a little while, until I get settled somewhere."

"You mean, like Texas?"

Annie rolled her eyes. "I'm not moving to Texas."

"David thinks you are."

She tensed at the mention of the other man's name and then smiled smartly. "Well, he's wrong."

Mitch laughed. "About some things, he certainly is. And of course you can stable your horse here for as long as you need."

They chatted for a couple of minutes and once she'd worked out a day and time for Mitch to collect Star and bring him to the Triple C, she thanked her brother-in-law and headed inside. Tess was upstairs in the nursery with her son and Annie tapped on the door frame before she entered.

"Hey, I'm so glad you're here," Tess said, smiling broadly. "I think Charlie just said *Momma*."

Annie laughed. "I thought *Dada* was his favorite word?"

"Not anymore," Tess replied and laughed.

"Mitch will be devastated," Annie teased.

"He'll get over it," Tess said, still smiling. "So, how are things?"

Annie gently touched the baby's head. "Complicated."

Tess had finished nursing and placed the child in Annie's arms. She sat down, gently cradling the baby.

"Which means?" Tess asked.

She drew in a long breath and spoke. "David proposed to me last night."

It sounded ridiculous and she watched as her sister stared at her in utter shock. *"What?"*

Annie nodded. "He asked me to marry him."

Tess's eyes were as wide as saucers. "And what did you say?'

"No," she replied. "Of course."

Tess smiled gently. "I thought you might…you know…"

Annie shook her head. "I might what?"

"Give it some consideration."

Annie looked at her sister. "I'm not that desperate."

"To marry the man you love?" Tess suggested.

"To marry a man who doesn't love me back," she replied and blinked back the heat burning behind her eyes. "David wants everything to stay the same because he hates change. I'm not going to go along with some plan he's concocted simply because it makes sense to his unromantic brain."

Tess regarded her kindly. "I guess it might *seem* like that. But perhaps—"

"Oh, no," Annie said and waved a hand. "I'm not going to start imagining there are any buts in this situation. David doesn't care about me in that way and one little kiss doesn't—"

"Whoa," Tess said quickly, eyes widened. "What kiss?"

Color crept up Annie's neck. "It was nothing. It happened days ago and—"

"Days ago?" Tess inquired, cutting her off. "And you're only mentioning it now?"

She shrugged. "It didn't mean anything. We were arguing and then it…happened."

"And afterward?"

"David apologized."

"Ouch," Tess said and grimaced. "So, it was only a kiss? Nothing else happened?"

Annie raised a brow. "You mean did I jump his bones? No, of course not."

Her sister sighed. "And missed the perfect opportunity."

Annie's skin heated. "I'm not wired that way. And I'm not about to start imagining it was anything other than a reckless, spur-of-the-moment thing on his part. All I have to do is get through the next two weeks and then I'm out of there."

Her sister looked at her with a gentle expression. "You're hurt by it?"

She nodded. "I'm not going to start fantasizing that this is anything other than him wanting to make sure his children are looked after by someone who loves them. David doesn't look at me that way. He doesn't really...*see me, if that makes sense.*"

"If he kissed you," Tess reminded her, "then I'm pretty sure he sees you."

"It didn't mean anything."

"Are you sure?" Tess asked gently. "Look, I understand why David would want to be with someone who loves his kids. I mean, I'd do anything to protect Charlie and make sure he's safe and loved. And maybe, in his way, David does—"

"He doesn't," Annie said quickly, preempting her sister's words. "I've turned his world upside down by quitting, and the best way he thinks he can fix the situation is by offering me a loveless marriage of convenience. Well, I can't accept those terms when I want more." She looked down at her sleepy nephew. "I want what you and Mitch have. And I know I deserve that."

She would never agree. Never settle. And never let him know how much she wanted to say yes.

On Wednesday afternoon David got home to find Mitch's horse trailer by the tables, and Annie bringing Star through the corral gate.

"I didn't expect you today," he said as his cousin approached and shook his hand.

"I'm boarding Annie's horse for a while," Mitch explained. "I thought you knew."

"I forgot," he replied, his stomach sinking.

As he spoke, Annie noticed him and immediately averted her gaze, loading her horse up the ramp. Once she was done, Mitch closed the tailgate and bolted it securely in place.

"Thank you," she said to his cousin, ignoring David.

"No problem," Mitch replied. "I'll take good care of him. I'll get him settled in and call you later to know how he's doing."

She thanked him again, glancing briefly toward David. "I'm going to see to the kids," she said. "They want to watch the kittens play."

She walked off toward the stables, hips swinging, her head at a tight angle.

"Things a little frosty around here I take it?" Mitch said and grinned once she had disappeared.

"A little."

"Got anything you want to tell me?"

David's gut sank. "I guess Annie told Tess, and your wife told you."

"I heard something about a marriage proposal."

David's back straightened. "It was just a—"

"You know, you can't expect to put a ring on the finger of a woman you haven't even taken on a date."

"We've been out together plenty of times," David replied, desperate to ignore the heat clawing at the back of his neck. "In fact, last Friday we went to JoJo's and—"

"I mean without two kids or a couple of grandparents as company," Mitch said, cutting him off again. "And anyway, the last time we talked about this, you said you and Annie didn't think about each other in that way and it was a ridiculous idea."

He shrugged. "I know what I said."

"What changed your mind?"

David sighed. "I...don't know," he said, unable to articulate the thoughts in his head. "The kids don't want to lose Annie and she said she wants to get married. So I just...did it. It made sense at the time."

"And now?"

He shrugged again. "Does it matter? She said no, end of story."

Mitch laughed and slapped him on the shoulder. "Man, you're so screwed. Look, David, I have to get going, but let me give you some advice. I know you mean well, I do. Go with that. Just try not to be too..." Mitch sighed. "Try to put yourself in her shoes and think about how she feels. Okay? Annie *is* my wife's sister, remember? We don't want to be in the middle of your romantic entanglements."

"Then stay out of it," David said irritably. "I know what I'm doing."

"You sure about that?" Mitch asked, more seriously. "Looks like all you're doing is hurting someone we all care about."

"I'd never hurt Annie," he said flatly, conscious of how the very notion made his insides vibrate with a kind of uneasiness he wasn't used to.

"Glad to hear it," Mitch replied. "Maybe you should have thought about that before you asked her to marry you just because it *made sense at the time*."

David ignored the other man's gibe and once Mitch left, considered joining his family in the stables but then decided against it.

He headed back to the house, a heavy feeling pressing down on his shoulders.

Soon enough it was Friday again. He was at work, trying to concentrate. Annie was leaving in a week. The new nanny started on Monday. A new routine would be set. Usually he liked routine and order. But nothing about his current situation gave him comfort.

He checked his watch. Two fifty. Time to go and pick up Jasper from school. He'd made arrangements with Annie that morning, as he'd promised his son they could go to the store and purchase cat collars for the kittens. Three, since David had been conned into keeping three out of the litter. The other four were already promised to good homes, thanks to Annie.

Annie…

He'd barely seen her all week, and certainly hadn't repeated the marriage proposal offer. The truth was, he'd lain as low as he could, not exactly avoiding her, but steering clear of any real confrontation.

David had spent most of the week hanging out with the kids as much as possible. Annie, too, he knew, lingered when she said good-night or when she helped Jasper with his homework or read a story to Scarlett at bedtime. They'd met the new nanny, Mrs. O'Connell, and seemed to like her well enough, but both kids were clinging to Annie more than usual.

It was five o'clock by the time they arrived home, and after dropping a stack of files into his office, he headed to the kitchen. Jasper had already raced to the stables to show Rudy the kitten collars with instructions to be back in ten minutes. His grandmother and sister were behind the counter, decorating a large blue-and-white cake, and Scarlett was sitting at the counter beside Ivan, happily licking a wooden spoon smothered in frosting. David kissed his daughter's head and accepted the coffee cup Leah passed him across the counter.

"Are you okay?" she asked him, one brow up.

"Fine," he lied. "Cake looks good."

"It's the trial cake for Charlie's christening," Mittie said.

"Can we still eat it?" Ivan asked and grinned.

"Not until I send a few photos to Tess and we get

a thumbs-up," Leah said and chuckled and started taking snapshots on her phone.

Jasper came in through the back door and once he showed off the kitten collars, hung around the counter, ogling the cake.

"Can we eat it before dinner, Dad?" he asked.

"Not a chance, sport," David said and grinned, then cleared his throat a little. "Ah...is Annie around?"

"She's packing," Leah said quietly, clearly aware that the kids were listening. "I said I'd watch Scarlett for a while."

"I hate that Annie's leaving," Jasper said unexpectedly and then hiccuped.

Me, too...

And he also hated that he'd made such a fool out of himself with his idiotic proposal. Of *course* she'd refused him. The very idea was ludicrous. He should never have done it. But...seeing her with the kids, witnessing her affection for them, had done something to his judgment. It had addled his brain. Plus, she was so damned beautiful he couldn't think straight when he was around her. It was panic, that's all. A lapse in his good sense.

"I love Annie," Scarlett said, pouting. "I'm gonna miss her so much."

Me, too...

David caught the breath in his throat. *What is wrong with me?* He'd been in love—he knew the feeling. Love was easy and didn't give a person sleepless nights. Love wasn't about being angry, or resentful or plain old disappointed. Love didn't hurt. But losing Annie to some online boyfriend did. A lot.

"We all love Annie," Leah said and tried to smile, pointedly looking in David's direction. "But sometimes," she said and looked back toward Jasper, "people have to leave."

"Like Mommy did?" his son asked, clearly unhappy.

David took Jasper's hand and led him to the table, gently gesturing him to sit. He sat beside his son and held his small hand steady between his palms. "Your mommy loved you and Scarlett more than anything and she didn't want to go away. And Annie doesn't want to leave you, either. She just has things she has to do. And she can only do them if she leaves."

"What kind of things?"

"Grown-up things," David said and ruffled Jasper's hair and then hugged him affectionately. "It'll be all right—I promise. I'm here, your great-grandma is here, so are Pop and Aunt Leah. Now, how about you go and get cleaned up for dinner and afterward we'll have some cake?"

Jasper nodded and quickly disappeared from the kitchen. Once he was out of sight, Leah spoke.

"He's taking it so hard."

"I know. But he has all of us. He'll get through it," David said, knowing he sounded cold, but also knowing he had to keep his resolve and not show how torn up he was. "He has to."

"What about you?" his stepdad asked. "Will *you* get through it?"

David shook his head. "Don't start."

"I can't believe you're actually gonna let her go," Ivan said quietly.

"It's her decision," he said and ignored the sudden pounding at his temple. "Frankly, I'm tired of talking about it," he said and quickly left the room.

Thirty seconds later—despite knowing he was asking for trouble—he tapped on Annie's door.

It opened soon after and he noticed she was breathing hard.

"Everything okay?"

"Nothing an extra ten inches of height wouldn't fix," she said and pulled her sweater onto her shoulder after it slipped down.

David did his best to ignore the action. "What?"

"I can't reach the shoeboxes on the top shelf in my wardrobe."

"Would you like some help?"

She hesitated for a moment and then shrugged. "Sure."

David followed her through to the bedroom and immediately he was bombarded by a voice in his head telling him to turn around and leave.

"Up there," she said and pointed inside the wardrobe. "Top shelf."

He stepped inside the large wardrobe and the

scent of her perfume hit him with an almighty force. He reached up and extracted four shoeboxes.

"Is that it?" he asked and swiveled in the small space.

She was close. And the sweater had slipped again, exposing one smooth shoulder, and he couldn't look away. He wanted to kiss her there. Hell, he wanted to kiss her everywhere. Her mouth, her neck, her breasts. He wanted to plunder her mouth with his own, to feel her against him, to taste her sweet lips, to feel her tongue, her sighs, her breath. He wanted it so much his hands tingled and his stomach churned.

David met her gaze and saw the awareness in her expression. There was no denying it, no hiding it and no way, he suspected, of trying to diffuse it. He couldn't help but wonder how long it had been there between them—if it had been there all along and was just waiting to be fanned into life.

"I should go."

She nodded, stepping back. "Did you want to see me about something? I know I'm officially still on duty, but Scarlett wanted to help Leah and Mittie with the baking and Jasper was with you so I—"

"I don't watch your clock-in and clock-out times, Annie," David said and dumped the shoeboxes on the bed. "I thought you might want to spend some time with the kids tonight, that's all. Maybe watch a movie."

"I should keep packing..." she said, her words trailing off.

David saw the boxes scattered around the room. It added another layer of finality to the situation. The mood between them was tense and uncomfortable and his foolish proposal was an elephant in the room. And they both knew it.

"I just thought since Mrs. O'Connell starts next week and the kids will be spending time with her, that you might want to have some alone time with them."

"Oh…you mean…you won't be…"

"I mean I'll make myself scarce so you can relax and enjoy your time with them. Let's face it, we've managed to avoid each other most of this week."

She inhaled heavily. "I didn't want to talk about it."

"It?" he queried. "My marriage proposal? Well, for what it's worth, I'm…sorry."

"You are?"

He nodded. "I shouldn't have blurted it out like that last week. It was…insensitive of me. I guess I wasn't thinking rationally and didn't consider how it would come across. I know I'm not the most romantic guy in the world, but…well, it kind of made sense in my head at the time."

"But not now?" she asked, her eyes flashing.

He shrugged uncomfortably. "I'm realizing I didn't think about how it would make you *feel*."

David reached out and grasped her hand, finding her skin warm to the touch. She didn't pull away.

Didn't do anything other than stand still and look at him. "Annie...try not to be mad at me, okay?"

"I'm not mad," she said and rested her palm over his hand.

"Promise me you won't do anything rash?"

"Rash?"

"Like run off with your fireman," he said, feeling the effect of her touch race through his blood like a wildfire. "Not until we've... I don't know...sorted out this *thing* between us."

"There's nothing between us except four years of you signing my paychecks. Anything else you're suggesting is only there because it suits. I can't make any promises. I'm leaving and you've hired yourself a new nanny and life will go on." She removed her hand and stepped back, pulling free of his grasp. "So, that's it, David. Thank you for being a good employer."

His insides contracted. "Annie, don't—"

"You have to let me go," she said breathlessly, taking another step back. "Please don't make this any harder than it already is."

She walked away and as her silhouette disappeared through the doorway, David experienced a sharp pain deep in his chest, recognizing it exactly for what it was. Hurt. Grief. Loss. Things he'd experienced before. Things he'd programmed himself to never consciously feel again. But the sense of solitude he felt in that moment was paralyzing.

Annie was leaving and he would have to face life without her.

A fact that made him feel so lonely he could barely breathe.

Chapter Eight

Leaving the McCall ranch was one of the hardest things Annie had ever done. With her car packed and the remainder of her belongings being stored at the Triple C, Annie said her goodbyes to the kids, feeling as though her heart was being torn out from her chest. Scarlett clung to her and the new nanny, Mrs. O'Connell, had to gently unwind the child's arms from around Annie's waist. Jasper was subdued, but he held on to her for a long time. Mittie, Leah and Ivan all hugged her. And David shook her hand.

Shook her hand?

Everyone noticed. How could they not? And she wondered, as she watched them all in turn, if they had guessed the real reason why she was leaving.

David, of course, had no clue. He'd stopped asking. The truth was, *they'd stopped talking.* The final week had been the hardest, with handing over the reins to Mrs. O'Connell and feeling the kids' unhappiness through to the marrow in her bones. Annie had spent all her time either with the new nanny, the children or holed up in her room avoiding him.

She waved as she drove off and burst into tears the moment she turned out of the driveway.

The O'Sullivan Hotel was a good place to relax and refocus. She'd booked herself a suite, with a small balcony and a great view of the Black Hills. Her first night had been strange, like she was vacationing somewhere and would soon go back to her real life. Realizing the hotel, and the current situation, *was* now her real life, had a polarizing effect and she spent most of Saturday morning walking around the suite in a daze, drinking tea, ordering room service, thinking, napping and dreaming.

Late Saturday afternoon her cell rang and Byron's familiar voice quickly made her smile.

"Hey, beautiful!"

He always called her that. Always made her feel good about herself. He was a nice man—someone she could potentially fall in love with.

If she gave him the chance.

They talked for a few minutes about the weather and his parrot named Waldo, before he suggested they meet up. Again.

"Now you've left your job there's nothing holding you back, right?" he asked.

"Yes, nothing," she agreed, knowing she was still in love with her ex-boss and that she needed time to get over it, if she even could. But she didn't say that to Byron. "We'll set it up soon, I promise. I have a couple of job interviews in Rapid City lined up early next week," she said and explained about the two admin positions she'd recently applied for and had been successful in securing interviews for.

"You know, there are jobs in Texas," he said and chuckled. "In fact, there's a part-time receptionist job going at the fire station. Wouldn't that be great? We could see each other all the time."

She longed to share his enthusiasm. "We'll see, okay."

"You'd love it here. Texas is all heart."

Like he did, she suspected. There was something open and earnest about Byron. He wasn't afraid to talk about feelings. On paper he was the perfect guy. The only thing was, Annie wasn't sure he was the perfect guy for her.

"Tell me, how was the interview?" her sister asked on Tuesday afternoon when she called.

Annie held the cell close to her ear and dropped into the sofa. "It was good. I'll know more next week. How's Charlie?"

"Perfect," Tess said. "Don't forget the christening on Saturday."

"Of course I won't. I'm looking forward to it. I bought a new dress."

Her sister was quiet for a moment, and then sighed. "Are you really okay?"

Annie swallowed hard. "I miss the kids a lot," she admitted, her insides crunching.

"I'm sure they miss you, too."

The ache in her chest amplified. For days she'd had a pain deep down, and knew it was grief. She missed Scarlett and Jasper so much it hurt. "I feel like I've abandoned them," she said, admitting it to herself and her sister for the first time. "And like a piece of my heart is missing."

"You love them," Tess reminded her. "It's natural you'd feel this way. Do you regret turning down David's proposal?"

"No," she replied quickly. David didn't love her. Sure, she believed he cared, and they had become friends over the years—but that was all. And it wasn't enough. It would *never* be enough. "I don't want that kind of marriage. I need more than that, Tess. You know David doesn't love me."

"Are you sure?"

"Positive," she replied, her heart heavy. "And he never will."

Once she ended the call with her sister, Annie took a shower and changed into her favorite jeans, a bright silky blouse and her boots. She was meeting Leah for a drink at the bar in the hotel that evening and was about thirty seconds into their conversation when she asked about the kids.

"They're fine," her friend said and sighed. "But they miss you. We all miss you."

"I miss you, too."

"David's unbearable at the moment," Leah said and grinned as she sipped her pineapple daiquiri. "Worse than we expected. My brother is an idiot."

Annie wasn't going to disagree, but also didn't want Leah imagining something was going on between them. Because it wasn't. One brief kiss and a marriage proposal aside, she and David were not any kind of *thing*.

"He likes his life in order, not chaos," she reminded Leah. "Once he gets a new routine it will be situation normal."

"He's in love with you, Annie," Leah said bluntly. "Everyone can see that. I mean, everyone but my stupid brother."

Her heart almost stopped. "He's not and I don't –"

"And you're in love with him, too," the other woman said, gentler now.

"I'm not," she denied swiftly. "And I hope you won't say anything to—"

"Of course, I won't," Leah said and smiled gently. "You're my friend and I want to see you happy. If he's too blind to see how wonderful you are, then he doesn't deserve you. But," she added and winked, "if he does come to his senses, promise me you'll consider it, okay? You're my friend and even though

I don't understand why you'd want to be with a stick-in-the-mud like my big brother, if he does manage to work it out, there's nothing I'd like more than to call you my sister-in-law."

Annie's throat burned with emotion and being with Leah made her miss the McCalls more than she already did.

Declining a second drink, she hugged Leah goodbye around seven o'clock, saying she'd see her at the christening on the weekend.

Early on Thursday morning Annie showered and changed into fresh jeans and a shirt, grabbed her jacket and headed downstairs. The foyer was busy and she waved to a couple of people she knew as she headed out into the morning sunshine and walked down the street. The sidewalk was spotted with people and she made eye contact with a few she recognized and headed for the bakery down the block. And of course, after almost six days of *not* seeing David, he was the first person she saw when she entered the store. He was sitting at one of the tables, head down, glasses perched on his nose, his concentration taken by the laptop on the table. He wore a suit, pale blue shirt and one of the ties she'd gifted him and looked utterly gorgeous. He had one hand loosely around a take-out coffee cup and the remnants of some kind of pastry on a plate he'd pushed aside. His left hand—the one without the wedding ring. She wondered for a moment about why he'd suddenly taken the band off. Perhaps to make a point? That he was available. That he was ready to get married again. In body, perhaps. But not his heart. Leah was wrong. He didn't love her. Not the way she needed to be loved. He liked her. He respected her. And yeah, he cared. But not enough— and not the way she needed him to.

Annie considered bailing, but she knew she couldn't avoid him. Cedar River was a small town and chances were, she'd run into him occasionally. The two jobs she'd applied for were in Rapid City – which would be better. It was close enough that she could visit Tess, but far enough away that she wouldn't see David on every street corner. Or bakery.

She considered being a coward for about ten seconds and then spoke. "Hello, David."

His head jerked up and he stared at her, looking way too sexy in his dark-framed glasses and slightly tousled hair. "Annie. Hi."

She gripped the back of the chair. "How are the kids?"

"Fine," he replied and straightened up the papers in front of him. "They miss you."

Of course he would say that. Anything to make her feel bad. "I miss them, too. How's the new nanny working out?"

"Very efficiently," he said quietly. "How do you like staying at the hotel?"

She shrugged a little. "It's okay."

"I'm surprised you're not staying with Tess."

"She asked," Annie said and motioned to the chair. "But I wanted some time alone."

He nodded, like he understood. "Would you like to join me?"

"No," she said quickly and realized how desperate she sounded, then shook her head. "I mean, I don't want to disturb you if you're working."

"I'm not," he said, closed the laptop and got to his feet. "I'll get your coffee. Decaf hazelnut latte with extra foam, correct?"

He actually knew what coffee she liked?

Maybe he has been paying attention...

When he returned to the table he had a take-out cup in one hand and a small brown bag in the other. He passed her both items and sat down.

"What's this?" she asked.

"Your favorite pastry."

Annie looked inside the bag and spotted a peach Danish, ignoring the way her insides fluttered a little. "Thank you. Although I've already had breakfast."

"What about dinner?"

She stared at him, eyes widening. "Dinner?"

"Tomorrow night," he replied, his gaze unwavering.

"I don't think I should see the children just yet," she said and swallowed hard. "It's probably too soon and they will only get confused and—"

"Child-free," he said, cutting her off. "Just you and me."

Annie straightened her already straight back. He could mean only one thing, right? "Um…you mean, like a date?"

"Exactly like a date." He held her gaze.

David wanted to take her on a date? Shock vibrated through her and she stared at him. "I'm not quite sure what to say."

"Yes would be a starting point."

She hesitated, thinking about all the reasons why she shouldn't. About her reasons for leaving. About her plans for a life post-David. About Byron. About everything. And then caved. "Sure."

"I'll pick you up at the hotel at six thirty," he said and quickly placed the laptop into his satchel and cleared away the cup and plate. "See you tomorrow," he said with a smile, and left without another word.

Annie remained where she was for a while, sipping her latte, thinking about what she'd just agreed to and wondering if she hadn't completely lost her mind. She had a date with David. Perhaps he wanted to talk about the kids. Or maybe the new nanny wasn't working out and he wanted her thoughts. Whatever his reasons, it couldn't be a *real* date.

Because thinking it was would only lead to her heart breaking more than it already was.

David headed to the kitchen late on Friday afternoon and spotted Leah standing behind the countertop, adding the final touches to the christening cake. Apparently, Tess had heartily approved of the sample. He watched as she decorated the top of the blue and white concoction while Scarlett played with a few candied flowers he suspected were supposed to be for decoration. Leah looked up and smiled when he entered the room.

"You look nice," she said and raised a brow. "Hot date?"

He ignored the heat settling under his collar. "Maybe. We'll see."

Leah's brows shot up. "Annie?"

He shrugged, staying noncommittal. "It's just dinner."

She nodded. "Gotta start somewhere."

"Thanks for watching the kids."

"My pleasure," she said and grinned. "At least one of us is getting out."

"I thought you'd sworn off dating after the last debacle with what's-his-name?" he queried and laughed softly, thinking that reminding Leah about her no-good ex probably wasn't his smartest move.

"I have," she replied. "Love sucks. But a date every now and then would be okay. Except I'd have to deal with the inevitable groping at the end of the evening by some oversexed Neanderthal."

He looked at his sister, reading between the lines of her words. Leah was essentially a cheerful person, but he knew her last breakup had been messy and left her having serious trust issues. "There's someone special out there for you, Leah."

"Maybe." She shrugged. "And for you?"

"Time will tell, I guess."

"Don't wait too long to make your move," Leah said and winked. "Someone else might be waiting in the wings to snatch *she-who-we-don't-dare-mention* up."

The heat under his collar intensified and he wondered if Leah knew something he didn't. "You mean the fireman?"

Leah nodded fractionally. "She's not going to wait forever for you to come to your senses."

"Is that what she's doing?" he asked, suddenly hopeful. The truth was, the last week had been crappy and he knew it was because he missed Annie so much. He missed her laughter around the house, he missed the soft sound of her voice as she spoke to his children, he missed the scent of her perfume lingering throughout the house long after she returned to her room each evening. And he missed the way she made him feel. Seeing her at the bakery had only confirmed what he already knew—and made a mockery of what he'd made himself believe for the past four years. That he didn't see her as simply the nanny. He saw her as a woman. A woman he was attracted to. A woman he didn't want to see in the arms of another man.

But he wasn't ready to pin a name on his emotions. However, the more he thought about marriage, the more he realized it was the right thing. The only thing. He could make it work.

"Annie's my friend, David. I care about her."

"I care about her, too," he said.

"I know," Leah supplied. "The point is, how much."

David's gut sank. It was a good question. Enough to marry her? Enough to be a caring, devoted husband? Enough to give her what she wanted – a family of her own? He hoped he was ready for that. All he knew is that he didn't want to give up without a fight.

Leah shooed him from the kitchen. "Go. I'll look after the kids. And David," she added as he went to leave. "Try to be charming."

He scowled. "I'm always charming."

She laughed. "I mean, don't be an uptight know-it-all. Just, I don't know…chill out. Relax a little."

He headed into town and found a parking space near the hotel entrance. It was just before six thirty when he spotted Annie standing in the hotel foyer, looking so beautiful in a midlength black dress and heeled black boots that he almost buckled at the knees. Her hair was down and fell across her shoulders. She half smiled when she saw him and walked across the foyer, her hips swaying.

"You look lovely," he said and touched her elbow, frazzled by the shot of electricity that raced up his arm when his skin connected with hers. "Nice dress."

"Thank you. Where are we going?"

"The honky-tonk place just out of town. Unless you'd prefer to stay here?"

"No," she replied. "I've never been there and I hear they do barbecue ribs to die for."

David grinned. "I've heard the same thing."

She looked at him curiously. "You've never been there, either?"

David's gaze lingered on her. "Nope."

She waited until their eyes met before replying. "I thought you might have taken what's-her-name."

David was halfway to opening the passenger door and looked at her. "Rachel? We broke up," he reminded her.

She nodded. "Mmmm."

"She was a vegan."

"She had nice legs," Annie said as she got into the BMW.

David held the door ajar and chuckled "I don't remember. Besides, legs aren't really my thing."

"No?" Her brows shot up. "What's your *thing*?"

Heat tugged at his collar. Be damned if it didn't feel as though she was flirting. "I'll be sure to tell you sometime," David said as he closed the door and then moved around to the driver's side. Once he was in the car and buckled up, he started the ignition and placed both hands on the steering wheel. "You know, you're very sexy when you flirt."

"I'm not flirting," she denied and made a scoffing sound.

"Sure you are. And incidentally, I'm not complaining. Leah told me not to be a bore tonight, in not so many words."

Her head jerked sideways. "You told your sister we were going out?"

He nodded. "Was I not supposed to?"

"No, I mean…yes," she said quickly. "I wasn't expecting it, that's all. What did she say?"

"Not to be myself. Try to be charming."

Annie laughed. "Why do you need to be charming?"

"To fight off the competition."

"What?"

"My sister told me your fireman is getting serious," he said and turned the vehicle onto the highway. "Is that true?"

"He wants to meet."

David sucked in a breath. "Actually, I'm surprised you haven't already headed to Texas."

She was silent for a moment. "I'm still deciding. And what do you mean about the competition? Why would it matter to you? I thought you asked me out so we could talk about the kids."

"Nope."

He heard her hard swallow. "Then what?'

"Why does a man normally ask a woman out to dinner?" he challenged.

"So they can get to know one another," she replied.

"Exactly," David said.

"But we already know each other," she reminded him.

David glanced at her and then returned his eyes

to the darkened road ahead. "We have a working relationship. And we're friends," he added. "I'd like to change that."

"Why?"

"Because I want you to marry me, Annie," he said flatly. "But I realize I need to change my approach…to court you, so to speak."

"A means to an end, then?"

"You know me," he said, hearing the frustration in her voice. "I'm not flowery or romantic and don't believe in lying to get what I want."

"And you want me?" she asked bluntly. "Is that it?"

Heat prickled his skin. "Well…yes."

"That's kind of drastic, don't you think?" she shot back. "I mean, you have a new nanny now and I'm sure she'll turn out to be adequate at looking after the kids."

"They need more than adequate," he reminded her. "They need you."

"And you'd sacrifice yourself to make it happen?"

He glanced sideways, saw the way her jaw was wired tightly. "I'd hardly call marrying you a sacrifice, Annie."

"You remember what marriage is?" she inquired; both her brows rose and her lovely mouth set into a grim line. "You know, all the things you have to do."

"Sure," he said and shrugged a fraction, conscious of the heat crawling up his neck at the implied intimacy. "Hanging out together, arguing, making up, sleeping in the same bed."

"And pretending," she said quietly. "That you're now attracted to me."

"I wouldn't need to pretend."

She turned her head and laughed humorlessly. "Have you suddenly got sex blinkers on?"

"Sex blinkers?"

"The kind that make someone attractive because it suits you," she replied. "I hear they can become quite the burden over time. I wouldn't want you to get crushed beneath the weight of good intentions."

"Are you implying I've given you the impression that I'm not attracted to you?"

"Not implying," she said. "Stating a fact backed up by the way you've treated me over the last few years. I mean, I understand you needed time to grieve your wife's passing, but I also –"

"You're right,' he said, cutting her off. "I did. And I have. As for being attracted to you and how I have treated you these past few years – do you think it would have been appropriate to act on that attraction and chase you around the house?"

"Of course not," she said quickly. "You were my boss."

"Precisely. But I'm not now."

She let out a heavy sigh. "Marriage because your kids miss me isn't enough, David. I want to have a child of my own. I want to be with someone who—"

"We could have a baby," he said quickly. "If that's what you want."

"A sacrificial marriage *and* a pity baby. Wow… that's quite the offer. I'm overwhelmed by the sentiment. This is the kind of thing people write sonnets about."

Her sarcasm wasn't disguised and he took a moment to reply. "Okay, so maybe this isn't all about roses and romantic declarations from below a balcony. Frankly, I'm not a sonnet or balcony kind of guy. But it's real, Annie. It's about as real as it gets."

Annie stared straight ahead, her heart hammering behind her ribs so hard she was sure he could hear it. Although she wouldn't cave. She wouldn't allow herself to imagine there was anything more to David's proposal than wanting to make his kids happy. He was *that* predictable. And in a way, she understood. She just didn't agree. She remained silent, thinking she should probably tell him to turn the vehicle around and take her back to the hotel. She wasn't a coward and could certainly endure an hour or so of his company. It would, at the very least, cement in her mind how crazy his proposal was and that she was right to refuse him.

When they arrived at the restaurant, the parking area was full, so they made do with a spot along the edge. The music was loud and *very* country, and she made a face once they were out of the vehicle.

"You don't like country music," she remarked and grabbed her bag as he came around the car.

"But you do," he said with a grin and closed the door once she was on her feet. "Let's go."

The restaurant was huge and had been built to resemble a saloon, with wraparound porch and shuttered windows. He didn't touch her as they walked, didn't speak as they were shown to their table by a waitress dressed in red gingham. There was a band playing and at least a dozen people were boot scooting on the dance floor. It made Annie smile, particularly since she knew how David preferred more mainstream dining and jazz music. Because of that, she was impressed by his effort and said so once they sat down.

"I can do the cowboy thing when I need to," he said and looked over the menu.

Annie hitched a thumb in the direction of the dance floor. She knew David didn't dance. "Does that mean line dancing a little later?"

He quickly shook his head. "Ah—not on your life."

"You mean this isn't a full-service date?"

He fumbled with the cutlery and stared at her. "What?"

"Dinner *and* dancing." She raised one brow suggestively. "Did you think I meant something else?"

He cleared his throat. "Of course not. We've already established that you don't do anything casually—you told me so when you shot me down in flames."

"Is that what I did?" she asked.

"Absolutely," he replied. "Callous of you, I thought."

She laughed at his teasing, her mood lightening a little. "I'm sure your ego is healthy enough to take it."

The waitress arrived and she ordered a wine spritzer and David opted for a craft beer. When the waitress returned with their drinks, Annie decided against the ribs and ordered the chicken special and David settled on steak and salad.

"Have you thought about what you're going to say at the christening tomorrow?" she asked, trying to keep the conversation neutral. "Tess did ask us both to say a few words."

He nodded. "It's quite the responsibility. Jayne was an atheist so we never got Jasper or Scarlett baptized. I figured they could get it done when they're older if they wish to."

"I never knew that about her," Annie mused, then decided to dip her toe in a bit further. "You know, you don't talk about her a lot."

He shrugged. "It's a bit of a double-edged sword, I suppose. If I say too much, it can upset the kids. If I don't say enough…well, that can upset them, too. Since Scarlett has no memory of her, it's difficult for her to understand that Jayne *is* her mother. The truth is, the only mom my daughter has ever had, Annie, is you."

In her heart, Annie knew his words were true. "I never planned on loving them so much," she admitted.

He nodded. "I know. I guess, after Jayne and my mother died, I never planned that I'd find someone who was so easy for them to love. But I did. And it worked. My kids are well-balanced and happy and a real joy. And you are a huge part of that, Annie. I know you think I proposed because it would fix everything—and maybe at first that played into it." Her expression flared, but he put up a hand, gesturing that she let him finish. "But's it's not only that, I assure you. The truth is, I don't know how my kids can be happy or whole without you. And that terrifies me."

Annie sat perfectly still, watching him, seeing a vulnerability in his expression she'd never witnessed before. Sure, she'd seen him cheerful and irritated and impatient and amused. But this was different. This was raw and real. This was the David she'd always longed to see. But she couldn't compromise herself—not even for the children she cared for so deeply. She had to get him to understand. "It's you they need, David. And you're such a good father."

"I don't think I'm enough," he admitted.

"Of course you are," she assured him and touched his arm, feeling the muscles bunch against her palm. "And you said you wanted to spend more time with them? Isn't that why you hired a part-time nanny?"

"I did that because the idea of replacing you was inconceivable…and frankly, impossible."

His hand covered hers and the intimacy was excruciating. Annie looked down, noticing his bare ring finger…and for a moment, thinking how easy it would be to say yes. Yes to staying. Yes to marriage.

But she didn't. She couldn't. Not without love.

He removed his hand and so did she and when their meals arrived soon after, the tone of the conversation was much less dramatic for the next hour. But underneath the small talk, tension simmered. He looked so effortlessly handsome in his dark jeans, blue shirt and leather jacket. His hair was a little longer than usual and she wondered if he'd forgotten to get it cut. His glasses had slipped down the bridge of his nose and he pushed them up. Annie's heart rolled at the gesture and she quickly felt herself getting sucked back into his vortex…which was highly impractical since she'd spent the best part of her week talking herself *out* of having any feelings for David whatsoever. But proximity was a funny thing. And being so close, seeing the tiny crinkles around his eyes and the dimple in his cheek, was enough to set her feelings into overdrive.

She ate quickly, drank the remainder of her spritzer and declined dessert, anxious for the evening to end so she could resume her hibernation at the hotel and stop wishing for the moon.

"Would you like another drink?" he asked.

Annie listened to the slow country song now

being played by the band and shook her head, thinking that what she really wanted was to dance with him and feel his strong arms around her. Although David didn't dance. Not ever.

"Did you dance at your wedding to Jayne?"

He shook his head. "We got married at the courthouse and had a small reception afterward. Jayne wasn't much of a dancer, thankfully," he added with a rueful look. "She had two left feet, like me."

"You can't be that bad?"

He nodded. "I am. Isn't there something you're bad at?"

Falling out of love with you…

She shrugged. "I'm terrible at Scrabble."

"I know," he said and grinned. "I beat your pants off every time." He paused for a moment, his gaze settling on her mouth. "I mean…not literally."

The moment he said the words, Annie's skin scorched, because the image was too hot to contemplate. She managed a smile, despite the way her heart pounded. "I think it's time to go."

He nodded. "You're probably right."

He signaled to the waitress for the check and within minutes they were outside and walking through the parking lot. It was a cool night and when she shivered David automatically slipped off his jacket and placed it around her shoulders.

"Thank you," she said and felt warmth seep through to her bones.

She tripped on a pebble and David quickly

grasped her hand, steadying her. Her hand remained clasped within his until they reached the car and she waited as he opened the passenger door.

Conscious that he was directly behind her, she turned so she was facing him, tilting her neck to meet his gaze. The tension between them was palpable. The awareness hot and heady. It had been building all evening. No, she corrected…it had been building for weeks. Ever since they'd spent those couple of hours at the cabin by the river. Now here they were, alone, after a…date? It was crazy. Everything that had happened between them in the past few weeks bombarded her thoughts. Her resignation. The kiss. His proposal. It was emotional chaos on a giant scale, because for so long she'd lived emotionally sheltered, not giving any part of herself up, not falling in love, not living in her own *present*.

"Annie…"

He said her name on a whisper, moving closer, one hand moving around to gently cup her nape, and she shuddered, totally lost. "David…please…"

"Damn it, Annie," he rasped out, so close she could feel the warmth of his breath against her cheek. "I've tried to ignore my feelings for you, honestly I have. But I just can't do it anymore, and—"

"You're saying that to get what you want," she rushed back, swallowing hard, feeling his nearness envelope her like a cloak. "To get me to agree to marry you."

"I'm not," he assured her, his thumb drawing tiny

patterns on her neck. "I'm saying it because it's true. I didn't expect this to happen. I've programmed myself to look at and think of you a certain way. Now everything has changed." He sighed. "Tell me you feel the same."

What she felt was his body almost touching hers. "I do," she admitted breathlessly.

"Annie..." he said her name again, almost as though it pained him, and pressed his forehead against hers, the feeling startlingly intimate despite its chasteness. Then he pulled away. "I'll take you back to the hotel."

He moved, pulling away, and as their bodies parted Annie experienced an acute and immediate sense of loss. And suddenly, more than anything, she wanted his arms around her. She pressed closer and moved her hands to his shoulders, holding him steady. "David, please. Kiss me."

David moaned. "Kissing you won't be enough."

"I know," she breathed and clutched his shoulders. "But kiss me anyway."

Chapter Nine

David looked down into her lovely face, noticing every line, every sweet angle. There was something so incredibly sexy about her and as he took her mouth in a searing kiss, the sensation almost buckled him at the knees. She was pressed against him, her lovely curves soft against the hard angles of his chest. He deepened the kiss, and gently anchored her head with one hand. Leaning closer, he ran one hand down her side, lingered at the underside of her breast, felt her ribcage through the fabric of her dress.

"Annie," he whispered against her mouth. "Tell me to stop."

"I can't," she said and gripped harder, digging her fingers into his shoulders. "I don't want you to stop."

David pressed closer until they were leaning against the car, angling her head so their kiss could have the deepest contact. It had been a long time since he'd been intimate with anyone, but he knew that the feeling of having Annie in his arms was unlike anything he'd experienced before. She was soft and breathtakingly feminine and her breasts were pushed against him, driving him to distraction, turning his need into a desire that coursed through his blood like wildfire.

He ran a hand down her back, over her hip, and he bunched the dress in his hand, finding the skin soft beneath the fabric. He groaned, kissing her deeper, bringing his palm around the full curve of her bottom and drawing her closer. For a few crazy moments he didn't have enough air in his lungs or enough ground beneath his feet. All he could feel was Annie, the smooth skin beneath his palm, the erotic tease of her underwear against his fingertips. Never in his life had he felt such intense sexual desire. He wanted to touch her all over, to strip her bare and witness the flush across every inch of her lovely skin, to worship her breasts with his hands and mouth, to taste every dip and curve and find oblivion within the sweet depths of her body.

She groaned against his mouth and David trailed kisses along her jaw, then found a sensitive spot at the base of her throat. Her hands were in his hair, kneading his scalp, and she pushed her hips forward, coming into direct contact with his unmistakable arousal. More turned on than he ever had been in his life, David moved lower and touched her intimately, and the sensation made him ache with a kind of need he didn't know he possessed. She moaned, saying his name, pushing against his hand as he stroked her and he could feel her climax building when he heard a sound in the distance—a car door slamming, and a shot of laughter. Sanity returned and he realized where they were and what they were doing—making out, practically having sex, in the parking lot of a busy restaurant.

He pulled back quickly and removed his hand from beneath her dress, immediately straightening the fabric. She was breathing hard, staring at him with a mixture of shock and disbelief, her lips reddened from his kisses, her cheeks flushed, her breasts heaving, her hands shaking.

The inevitable groping at the end of the evening by some oversexed Neanderthal...

His sister's words came rushing back to him with appalling clarity and shame pressed down on his shoulders. He wasn't that guy. He'd never been that guy. He respected women. Okay, he'd slept with a few girlfriends over the years but ultimately married the only woman he'd ever loved. He definitely wasn't the guy who made out in a parking lot like a horny teenager.

Except, that up until about thirty seconds ago, he *had* been that guy.

"I'll take you back to the hotel," he said quietly,

fueled by a stab of self-loathing. He would never dis-respect Annie...he cared about her too much. But he had. Big time.

She was silent on the drive back to Cedar River and David was shamefully glad for the temporary reprieve. But he knew they needed to clear the air.

"Annie," he said as they pulled into the hotel parking area, "I think we should—"

"Good night, David," she said and grabbed the door handle.

"Do you want me to pick you up tomorrow?" he asked. "We could go to the christening together."

She shook her head. "I'm riding Star tomorrow, so I'll be at the Triple C early. I'll see you at the chapel."

"Annie," he said quickly, "can't we at least talk about—"

"No," she said tautly. "I don't want to talk about it. I want to forget this whole evening ever happened."

"How can we?" he asked, his chest so tight he could barely breath. "This is real, Annie. It's not just going to go away."

"Yes, it will," she said and took a long breath. "I can't believe you, David. I never imagined you would be the kind of man to toy with someone's feelings. Especially mine."

He went to touch her arm, to comfort her, but she pulled away. "I'm not, I promise you."

"You are," she said and shuddered. "You just don't know it."

She got out quickly and shut the door. He watched as she strode toward the hotel, then disappeared into the foyer. David remained where he was for a few minutes and then drove home. Once he was back at the ranch he checked on the kids, saw a note from Leah saying they'd gone to bed early and she was bunking in the spare room.

He took a shower, as cold as he could stand, and spent the next couple of hours staring at the ceiling. When he finally drifted off to sleep he was plagued by dreams of Annie and woke up late, groggy and feeling as though he needed to hibernate for a couple of days to set his mind straight. But he had things to do and a family who needed him, so he worked out for half an hour, then showered and at eight o'clock he got dressed and made his way to the kitchen. Stopping by to check on the kids, he found both of them up, still dressed in their pajamas and playing in their rooms. He chatted with each of them for a few minutes and then followed the scent of freshly brewed coffee down the hall.

Mittie was behind the countertop, scraping out leftover oatmeal from the kids' plates and Leah was perched on a stool, reading something on her cell phone.

His sister's brows rose curiously when she spotted him. "Rough night?"

He raised a dismissive hand. "I'm really not in the mood."

"Did you make things worse?" Leah asked, relentless.

Mitie tutted. "Can you two stop squabbling? Your brother hasn't even had any caffeine yet."

David grabbed a coffee mug. "Where's Dad?" he asked, noting that Ivan wasn't sitting at his usual spot at the table. "I thought he was coming over this morning?"

"He's not feeling well," Leah replied. "He texted me earlier and said he was going back to bed."

David frowned. "He's never sick."

She nodded. "I know. But he said he's been battling a headache for a few days and feels dizzy. You know Dad—he doesn't like to make a fuss. I'll stop by his place later and check on him. So, how was your date?"

"Fine," he replied. "Thanks for watching the kids last night. I'm going to take them to see their mom this morning."

Mittie's expression narrowed. "You haven't done that for a while."

"I know," he said soberly. "I don't want them to forget who their mother is."

"Jayne's in all our hearts," his grandmother said gently. "And I know she's in yours. That doesn't mean there isn't room for someone else."

David sighed. "I know. But the kids need to understand that Annie is not their mom and that she's not coming back here to work."

Half an hour later he bundled the kids into the BMW and headed for the cemetery. His wife was buried alongside her mother, who'd had her late in life and died when Jayne was in her teens. Her father was a professional card player and had abandoned his family when Jayne was a baby. She had no siblings, no real relatives who lived close, just an uncle and aunt who had moved to Ohio years ago. Looking at her gravestone, watching as the kids placed flowers there, David was overcome with an acute sense of loss and sadness. He missed her, but lately there were times when he couldn't quite recall what kind of marriage they'd had. Mostly happy, he believed. Although deep down, he knew he never quite understood Jayne's overwhelming need to be in the air. Sure, he'd loved her and supported her, but he also knew her passion for flying sometimes kept them emotionally as well as physically apart. And somehow, as he'd grieved for her over the last four or so years, he'd gotten on with the job of raising his children with someone else. Even if that someone else was on the payroll.

"Do you think Mommy misses us?" Jasper asked quietly, coming to David's side and grasping his hand.

"Yes, buddy," David said and swallowed the tightness in his throat. "I'm sure she does."

"I miss her, too," Jasper said. "Annie says it's

okay for me to talk to Mommy sometimes, even if Mommy doesn't answer."

"Annie's right," David said, aching inside.

Jasper sighed. "Maybe I should talk to Annie, too," he said. "Even though she's not living with us anymore." He paused. "I miss Annie reading me stories."

David crouched down and placed his hands on his son's shoulders. "I know you do. We all miss her."

As he said the words, David realized the truth in them. He missed her. And not simply because she looked after his children. But because she was integral to his family...and to *him*.

"I wish Annie was my mommy," Scarlett said and snuggled up next to them.

There were tears in his daughter's eyes and David swallowed the lump in his throat. Rather than give the kids some closure regarding their mother, bringing them to the cemetery had only amplified how much they missed Annie, their surrogate mom in nearly every way. The new nanny was efficient and accommodating, and a lovely woman, but he knew the kids would never feel the love from her that they needed. *A mother's love.* Like they'd received from Annie.

"How about we go into town and get some ice cream?" he suggested, trying to lighten the mood.

The kids agreed cheerfully and they spent an hour in Cedar River before heading back to the ranch to get ready for the planned celebration that afternoon.

The christening was scheduled for three thirty and they arrived at the small chapel in town in plenty of time. The pews were filled with family and friends and when he spotted Annie the air immediately rushed from his lungs. She looked lovely in a knee-length, pale green dress with matching shoes. Her hair was up, but the wispy bits falling around her temples were incredibly sexy. He left the kids with Leah and took his spot at the altar beside Annie, achingly aware of her as the familiar scent of her perfume assailed his senses every time she moved. The service was short and heartfelt and he was humbled that Mitch and Tess entrusted him with the role of godfather of little Charlie. He knew how hard their journey to parenthood had been, and how much their son meant to them.

Afterward, everyone headed for the Triple C, where Ellie, party planner extraordinaire, had arranged for a celebratory buffet beneath a tent near the small orchard. The event was reminiscent of his cousin Jake Culhane's wedding to Abby Perkins a few months earlier, and today it was a lovely way for the family to celebrate baby Charlie. And he knew, without a doubt, that Annie was avoiding him like the plague. She barely said two words to him during the chapel service and declined his offer to drive to the ranch together, even though the kids were overjoyed to see her and gave her hug after hug outside the chapel. Now they were back at the ranch and celebrating, and he watched her chatting with her friends with only one thought in his mind.

They really, really needed to talk.

All Annie wanted to do was figure a way to get David out of her stratosphere. And out of her thoughts. It didn't help that she could feel his penetrating gaze on her through the service at the chapel. Or when she was reunited with the kids after being away from them for a long and emotionally fraught week. But she didn't want to have a post-mortem about what had happened between them.

Well, what had *almost* happened.

As she held Charlie and spoke quietly to the crowd of friends and family about always being there for the child who had been entrusted to her care, Annie experienced an acute and gut-wrenching longing for a baby of her own. She didn't dare look at David. Didn't dare remember how he'd casually mentioned they could have a baby if she wanted one. Because the thought of having a child with him made her ache inside for all he was offering.

Ellie asked her to find the silver cake knife so they could cut the cake, which gave her an easy out from the celebration, a chance for a much-needed break, and she couldn't wait to get inside the house. Until she heard David's all-too-familiar voice saying her name. She stopped rummaging through the pantry drawers, straightened, turned and spotted him by the doorway, arms crossed, looking way too good for her peace of mind in a dark suit and bolo tie.

"What?" she snapped, her mouth pressed tight.

He didn't move. "We need to talk."

"I'd prefer it if we didn't," she said stiffly.

"Avoiding the issue isn't going to make it go away," he remarked. "What happened last night—"

"Is never going to happen again," she said, cutting him off. "All it did was—"

"Prove that it could work between us," he said, slicing through her protest. "Admit it, Annie, despite having just a working relationship for the last four years, there's something else going on now. We're clearly attracted to each other...there's no denying it."

She glared at him. "Seriously, your ego is bigger than Mount Rushmore."

"My ego isn't the issue," he remarked. "Your refusal to admit the obvious is."

"What's obvious?" she shot back. "That we made out for a few minutes?"

"It was more than that," he said and moved farther into the room. "I've made out before and it didn't feel like that."

"Like what?"

"Like me with my hand under your dress and you with your tongue in my mouth."

Annie gasped, turning hot all over. Put like that, it sounded hot and erotic. And exactly what it was—a couple of the most sexually charged minutes of her life. Of course, everything he'd just said was true. Desire and heat like that couldn't be faked. At least, not from a man like David. He wasn't a player and was discerning in his personal relationships. So yes, they had heat and attraction between them, but that alone wasn't enough to sustain a real relationship. Not when she was in love with him and he was only thinking about having her return to the ranch for the sake of his children.

"I'm not quite sure how to respond to that comment," she said flatly.

"With the truth," he replied. "That we have chemistry. A lot of it. And that we could make this work, if you'd give it a chance."

"It still doesn't change one obvious fact."

"And what's that?" he queried.

"That you've decided being together is what's logical and the upside is we'd probably have great sex."

"Not *probably*," he corrected. "And don't underestimate the power of great sex."

"I'm not sure I've ever had *great sex*," she shot back, her chest heaving, "so I wouldn't know the difference."

His gaze darkened. "Believe me, Annie, when we make love, you'll know the difference."

When...

She shuddered, feeling both aroused and then appalled. She could have jumped him right then and there, and might have if she hadn't heard a sound coming from the back door, and realized that Leah, Tess *and* Mitch were standing at the threshold, watching them and clearly hearing every word.

"Ah...sorry, guys," Leah said.

Mortified, Annie pressed a hand to her burning cheeks. "Excuse me, I have to go."

"Annie," David said quietly. "We're not done."

"*I'm* done," she assured him, glancing at the three people standing in the doorway. "I'm not a consolation prize, David. Not for you or anyone else."

He frowned. "That's not what this is about. I don't think that, not at all."

"Maybe not," she said and shrugged, a lump forming in her throat. "But it's how you're making me *feel*."

Annie left the kitchen and walked through the house, her entire body numb, her heart breaking. She grabbed her bag and keys on the way out, saying a quick goodbye to the kids before she stopped by the stables to spend a few moments with Star. Then she headed for her car, where she found her sister perched against the hood, arms folded, looking as though she wanted an explanation.

"You're running away?" Tess asked.

Annie opened the car and dropped her tote on the backseat. "I'm saving myself from heartbreak and humiliation. And I *really* don't want to talk about it right now."

Tess pushed herself off the car and moved around to the driver's side. "You know I support whatever choices you make. But I am worried about you, Annie."

"I know," she replied, smiling through her emotion, and hugged her sister hard. "But I'll be okay."

As she drove back into town, Annie thought about everything that had happened in the past few weeks and realized she needed to make some significant changes. Simply leaving the McCall ranch wasn't enough. Applying for work in Rapid City wasn't enough. If she wanted to truly change her life, then she needed to *embrace* that change. And that didn't mean giving in to her feelings for David every time they were together. It didn't mean allowing herself to be persuaded by his kisses. It meant distance. It meant allowing someone else in.

And that someone was Byron.

He always made her smile. He didn't have an ulterior motive in pursuing a relationship with her other that actually *wanting* a relationship. It was a win-win. Not one-sided. Not filled with agenda and compromise. All she had to do was take a leap of faith and give it a chance. It might, she realized, be the only way to erase David from her heart.

When she arrived back at the hotel, she grabbed her cell and called Byron's number.

It was definitely time to meet her fireman.

David was neck deep in work on Tuesday morning when he received a frantic call from Leah, saying that Ivan had collapsed. He was in an ambulance and on his way to the community hospital. It took David just seconds to shut down his computer and then head out to meet his sister in the emergency room as the EMTs were wheeling his stepdad into triage.

"I stopped by his house this morning," she explained, distraught and tearful and he hugged her close. "I found him on the floor in the kitchen. I don't know what happened or how long he'd been there. I spoke to him yesterday and he said he still wasn't feeling well." She shuddered. "I should have checked on him again last night."

"You couldn't know," David said soothingly, trying to hide the panic in his heart.

"I called 911 as soon as I got there and saw him," she cried. "God, I hope I wasn't too late."

"Did the EMTs give you any indication of what could be wrong?" David asked and led Leah toward a chair in the waiting area.

She shrugged. "Maybe his heart. I really don't know."

They stayed there for over an hour and finally a doctor emerged. David had known Kieran O'Sullivan since high school and was pleased Ivan was in good medical hands.

Dr. O'Sullivan sat down and explained the situation. "Your father has had a series of ischemic strokes, most likely several minor ones over the last couple of days. This morning he had a significant incident, which caused his collapse. He's resting now and you'll both be able to see him soon."

"I sense a but in this conversation," David said quietly, trying not to alarm his sister.

Kieran nodded. "He has some paralysis down his left side, and we will be monitoring him over the next few days to see if the strokes continue."

"He wasn't feeling well for the last few days," Leah said tearfully. "He was complaining of sore eyes and dizziness and he put it down to a migraine. I should have listened and—"

"You did everything right," Kieran assured her. "You called 911 and he was here well within an hour of being found. You probably saved your dad's life because you didn't panic and reacted so responsibly. He's lucky, and with care and therapy, I believe he'll recover from this."

Of course, they were relieved, but also knew Ivan had a long road to recovery ahead. He was a strong and independent man, and wouldn't take easily to being bedridden, infirm and perhaps in a wheelchair while he endured therapy to help regain the use of his left side. After talking with the doctor some more they were told they could see him within the hour.

David hugged his sister and was relieved when his cousins Jake and Joss arrived at the hospital. Having them on hand to help support Leah was reassuring. The Culhanes and McCalls were a tight-knit unit and were always there for one another in a crisis. And Ivan, even though he was a Petrovic, was very much one of them.

Leah cried as they headed into triage an hour or so later. Seeing Ivan, who was usually so strong and robust, looking so vulnerable, was hard for them all and he held on to his sister's shoulder, insisting that their dad would make it. When Mittie arrived Leah burst into tears and hugged his grandmother. Even though they weren't related by blood, the older woman was very much a grandparent to his half sister and was exactly the comfort Leah needed. David took a few moments outside of triage to contact the new nanny and keep her updated, and then spoke to Tess, asking her to watch the kids once the nanny left for the day.

It was after lunch when he headed for the hospital cafeteria, ordered coffee for everyone and was waiting by the window for his order when he felt a warm and reassuringly firm hand on his back. He turned and saw Annie in front of him. Seeing her made the tension pressing behind his ribs ease—and way more than he expected. She looked so lovely and so familiar—like a balm for the turmoil swirling through his system.

"Hi," she said simply.

"Hello."

"Tess called me," she explained and reached out, touching his arm. "I'm sorry, David."

He looked to where her hand lay and heat spiked

through his blood. Just a touch, he thought, and he was a goner. "Thank you for coming."

She nodded. "Is Ivan going to be okay?"

"We hope so," he replied and quickly ordered her the kind of coffee she liked and then told her about Ivan's collapse and the recuperation ahead.

"Let's sit down," she urged and pulled him toward the corner of the room to a small table.

David followed and sat down. "I'm so glad you're here. Leah would—"

"I know what Ivan means to you all," she said swiftly, her hand coming to rest against his on the table. "This must be difficult for you and your sister."

He let out a long and painful breath. "I'm so… I'm so…"

"What?" she prompted when his words trailed off.

David met her gaze and was drawn deeply into her eyes, and the words spilled from his lips. Words he'd never uttered before. "I'm so tired of loss."

She grasped his hand and linked their fingers in a startlingly intimate gesture. "I understand."

"I couldn't believe it, you know, when Jayne and my mom died," he admitted, swallowing the burning in his throat. "For the first couple of days I walked around in a daze. It's like, one moment they were there—my mom was in the kitchen, laughing at some silly joke of Ivan's, and Jayne was beside me, and we were talking about our next vacation, or the kids, or about something at work or she was explaining how she needed a landing strip on the ranch."

Annie's eyes widened. "I didn't think the ranch was big enough for that."

"It's not," he replied and sighed. "Strange, remember how I said the other day that we never argued—but we used to argue about that, all the time. I think I put the arguments out of my memory because I didn't want to feel guilty—or blame her in any way—or hold on to any bad feelings. And then...nothing. It was all over. No warning. No time to prepare. No opportunity to say goodbye. A police officer came to the house, told me the plane had gone down and that there were no survivors. It was like someone had cut my heart out. At first, I was so angry with her for leaving me. I kept thinking, *I have a four-year-old son and a newborn baby girl, so how am I supposed to do this alone?*"

"And yet, you did," she said generously.

He half smiled. "I haven't been doing it alone these last four years, Annie." He placed his other hand over their linked fingers. "And now, I've lost you, too."

"You haven't lost me," she said softly. "I'm right here."

Yes, he thought, but for how long?

Chapter Ten

The moment Annie heard about Ivan's condition she'd hightailed it directly to the hospital. She cared about Ivan and knew how much pain his family would be in. She knew Leah would be heartbroken. And she also believed David would be at his stoic best.

Yet, oddly, sitting with him in the cafeteria, she'd never before witnessed him being so raw and vulnerable. And it made her love for him intensify. Particularly because she knew there was nothing more she could do to comfort him and his family except be there.

The clerk behind the counter said his order was ready and once it was paid for, they headed back.

Annie waited with the Culhanes while David headed for triage to be with his grandmother and sister. Mitch arrived and Annie felt the incredible familial bond, confirming that the Culhanes and Mc-Calls were a big and robust family, clearly capable of shouldering any tragedy together.

It was nearly four o'clock before Ivan was transferred to the ward. She visited him for a brief moment, preferring to let the family be at his side. And then knew what she needed to do.

"I'll go back to the ranch and stay with the children," she said to David when they had a moment alone.

He frowned a little. "Tess said she'd—"

"My sister has her own baby to look after," she insisted. "The nanny clocks off at five thirty, correct?"

He nodded. "Yeah, but—"

"You stay here with Mittie and your sister and I'll take care of the kids," she suggested and squeezed his biceps. "You're needed here, David. Let me know how he is when you can."

David nodded and briefly touched her cheek. "Thank you."

Annie left the hospital and headed directly for the hotel. She showered, changed into fresh clothes, then called Tess from the road via speakerphone and assured her sister she was fine to watch the children until David returned.

"That's nice of you," Tess said.

"Don't read too much into it," she warned her

sister. "I care about Ivan and want to do what I can to help."

"I'm pretty sure that it's David you're thinking about right now."

Tess was right, but Annie wasn't about to admit to anything. She was needed, end of story.

He'd called Mrs. O'Connell and told her she was coming and the new nanny briefly voiced her concern about Ivan—although not enough to remain after she clocked off for the day. She was a nice woman, but the role was clearly only a job to her. It made sense, since she had children and grandchildren of her own.

The kids of course were delighted to see her, and she was immediately dragged into their rooms in turn to be shown their latest books and artwork.

Scarlett grabbed her tiara and waved it. "Annie, do you think Pop would like to wear my tiara? Remember when I had chicken pox and I wore it and got better?"

"I'm sure he'd like that a lot," Annie replied and took her hand, following Jasper to his room. Once they were there, Scarlett plonked herself in front of the fish tank.

"Is Pop going to be okay?" Jasper asked, biting his lower lip.

Annie sat beside him on the bed. "I think so. Your pop has a lot of people who love him and want him to get better. We just have to keep happy thoughts in our hearts, okay?"

"I'll try," he promised and then gave Annie a hug. "I always feel better when I talk to you."

"I'm glad," she said and blinked back the heat in her eyes. "You know I love you and Scarlett very much."

"I know," he said and smiled. "And you love Great-grandma Mittie and Pop and Aunt Leah, too?"

"Yes, absolutely."

Jasper looked at her, his mouth at an angle. "And do you love Daddy?"

Annie had no way of getting into a complicated discussion about love and feelings with an eight-year-old, so she didn't bother. "Of course I do."

For a moment, he looked as though he had the weight of the world on his little shoulders. "I wish you still took care of us, Annie. I wish things were the same."

Annie was tempted to offer some platitude about how life was about change and then realized the words would be more for herself than for the little boy she loved so much. She hugged him again and arranged bath time for both children before making a quick dinner of macaroni and cheese, followed by canned fruit with a dollop of ice cream. It was nearly eight by the time the kids were in bed. Scarlett fell asleep immediately, while Jasper dozed with a book in his hands. David had texted her after seven, saying he'd be home soon, but he didn't show up until after eight thirty. He looked tired and spent when he walked through the front door with Mittie.

"Leah's staying at Dad's, she said she needed to feed the cat," David said as they crossed the threshold. "Dad's okay," he added when Annie made a startled face. "Holding his own. He's awake, although he's having some trouble talking normally because of the paralysis. But he's good considering what he's been through. We'll know more in a couple of days once the doctors see how he responds to therapy."

"I'm beat," Mittie said and sighed. "I'm going to turn in," she added and hugged Annie. "Thank you for being an angel. I bet the kids were so happy to see you. The place certainly isn't the same without you. Good night, try to get some rest, David."

"I will, Nan."

Mittie disappeared down the hallway and her footsteps quickly faded when she reached her part of the house. Annie looked at David and smiled. "I should get going. The kids are in bed and you look like you need to—"

"I'm too wound up to sleep," he said and ran a hand through his hair. "But I need a shower, shave and a change of clothes. Then maybe we could hang out for a while. I just need... I think I just need to let off some steam, you know?"

"Are you hungry?" she asked. "I have some left over mac and cheese, or I could make a sandwich or something."

His gaze was intense behind his glasses. "A sandwich would be great. And coffee? I'll be back in fifteen minutes."

It was more like half an hour when he returned, looking refreshed and too gorgeous for words with his clean-shaven jaw, jeans, white T-shirt and loafers. Annie busied herself making the sandwich and coffee as he went around the counter and stood beside her.

"Thank you for watching the kids. I just checked in on Jasper and he said you talked to him about his grandfather—so thank you for that, as well."

She nodded. "It was nice to spend some time with them."

"I'm sure they appreciated it. The new nanny is—"

"An employee," she said without accusation, cutting him off. "And not...you know."

"Like you," he said quietly. "Part of the family. An important part," he added.

Annie's eyes burned. It would have been so easy to slip back into the routine that used to be her life. So easy to forget the very reason she left in the first place. Because she wanted the moon and would never be content with only the stars. Even if those stars came in the shape of David's amazing kids.

"Leaving them was the hardest thing I've ever done."

"I know."

"I didn't make the decision lightly."

"I know that, too," he said. "You said you had your reasons."

Because I love you, you big oaf.

"You sound as though you don't believe them," she remarked.

"That you want to get married and have a family?" he shrugged. "Sure I do. I get it. I just can't believe you'd want to do it with some guy you've never met."

Annie's cheeks burned. Because the only man she wanted to marry and have a family with was the one standing beside her. "I don't expect you to understand."

He went to say something, then stopped, saying something else instead, she was sure. "It's been quite a day," he said wearily and rested his behind on the counter. "Nan's right—you are an angel."

"I'm not sure I—"

"You were wrong the other day," he said, cutting her off with quiet intensity. "You're *not* a *consolation* prize, Annie. A first prize. And certainly much more than I deserve."

Annie sucked in a shallow breath, conscious of the sudden lack of space between them and the bald intimacy of his words. She kept her hands on the counter, palms down, breathing deeply. She looked at him, saw the way the pulse throbbed in his cheek and how his eyes appeared so brilliantly green behind his glasses. Without thinking, Annie reached up and touched his cheek, running her palm along his jaw. There was a rawness to his expression, as though the rest of the world didn't exist in that moment and there were only the two of them alone in the big kitchen, seeking solace and comfort within each other. And she knew, without a doubt, what she wanted.

"David…" She said his name on a long sigh.

"You should go," he said softly.

Annie nodded, still touching him. "Or I could stay."

He inhaled sharply. "If you stay, we'll make love."

"I know," she whispered.

"I don't want you to regret it tomorrow," he said, and gently grasped her hand, holding it tightly in his own.

"Right now," she said with a sigh, "I don't think tomorrow matters all that much."

"Annie," he chided, "think about what you're saying."

"I know exactly what I'm saying," she said and tugged on his hand, leading him from the kitchen, flicking off the light as she continued the journey left, down the long hallway and toward the privacy of the master suite. She didn't release his hand and didn't speak. Instead, she turned on the bedside lamp and switched off the main light. The room was large and intimidating, the huge king-size bed a beacon, teasing and tormenting.

Annie dropped his hand and stood by the end of the bed, watching him, thinking that he'd never looked so handsome, or so uncertain. She suspected she should have been the one who looked resistant, but oddly, all she felt was a sudden kind of easy calm.

"Are you sure about this?" he asked quietly.

Annie nodded and slipped off her shoes. "Completely."

He remained perfectly still, gazing at her, almost absorbing her with his eyes. Then he took a step toward her, closing the gap between them. He reached out and cradled her cheek, rubbing his thumb along her jawline until he reached her chin and then gently held her there.

"You're so beautiful, Annie," he said and traced his fingertips down her neck. "Inside. Outside. In every way that counts."

Heat traversed through her blood and pooled low in her belly. "Kiss me," she beckoned.

He groaned and drew her toward him, taking her mouth in a hot and searing kiss that defied reason and logic and any lingering protest either of them may have had. Annie felt his tongue in her mouth and moaned, pushing closer, longing to feel the hard angles of his body pressed against her own. She wound her arms around him, settling at his waist, opening her mouth a little more, letting him in, feeling both acquiesce and power, knowing he was as overwhelmed by the heat and intensity of their kiss as she was.

His hand smoothed down her side and over her

hip, while the other gently anchored her head and he continued to kiss her, continued the erotic foray in her mouth that was like nothing else she'd ever experienced. Need, bone aching and deep, surged through her limbs and across her skin; suddenly kissing wasn't enough—she wanted skin to skin, breast to chest, she wanted to feel him deep inside her, until there was no space between them, no way to work out where he began and she ended.

Annie thrust her hands beneath his shirt and came into contact with his smooth, warm skin. For so long she'd yearned to touch him, to feel the muscle stretched over sinew and bone, to give herself up to the love in her heart. In that moment, it didn't matter that he didn't love her in return. He *needed* her, and perhaps it would only be for a few hours, but she could be there for him. And she needed him, too.

He dispensed with the buttons on her sweater and pushed the fabric from her shoulders, trailing kisses along her collarbone, making her mindless, fueling the desire that was surging through her blood.

"Annie," he muttered, his breath warm against her skin, "tell me what you want."

His words were inflammatory and sexy, giving her confidence. "Everything," she whispered, finding his mouth again in a hot and searing kiss. "All of you."

He groaned, half pleasure, half pain, and led her toward the bed, halting when the backs of her knees met the mattress. He took off his glasses, placed them on the bedside table and then looked at her, watching as she breathed, as her full breasts rounded over the cups of her bra.

"Not legs," he said sexily and trailed his thumb between her breasts, reminding her of a conversation they'd previously had. Her nipples hardened instantly, peaking against the smooth satin fabric and he moaned again, clearly aroused. "I want you so much, Annie. I can't even begin to say the words."

"I think you're saying them just fine," she said and smiled warmly. "With your kiss, and your eyes, and…" her words trailed off as her hands moved to the belt securing his jeans, lingering there for a moment before she met his burning gaze, "everything else."

He kissed her again and then stepped back, ditching the T-shirt and quickly flipping off his loafers. Annie stood silently and eased down the zipper and the back of her skirt, letting the fabric pool at her feet. Standing there in front of him, in only her underwear, she had never felt more provocative, or as desired in her entire life. She looked at him, absorbing the hard angles of his body, thinking about how many times she'd seen him without a shirt over the years and how this time she was allowed to look, allowed to feel, allowed to touch. She was allowed to love him, even if it wasn't real and wouldn't last beyond a few hours. And for the moment, that was enough.

* * *

In all his life, David knew he would never forget how Annie looked standing in front of him. The stretchy fabric of her panties dipped over her hips, highlighting every lush curve, filling him with the kind of aching desire he hadn't expected to feel. A desire that had everything to do with the fact it was Annie, and not just anyone. She meant something to him. She was special.

Her skin was smooth and supple, pale in places where it didn't see the sun. He watched as her hands moved around to her back and she unclipped the bra and then slipped off her panties. He swallowed hard, mesmerized by her, thinking how she reminded him of some ancient goddess from an old painting, all curves and femininity.

She stepped toward him and touched his ribcage, then teased her fingertips along his pectorals and settled lower at this belt for a moment. She stilled, seeming a bit uncertain.

"Are you okay?" he asked softly.

She looked up. "A little out of practice."

"Me too," he said. "But I'm sure we'll do just fine."

She smiled again, warmer, deeper and then with a dexterity that startled him, she unbuckled the belt with agonizing slowness, undoing the zipper on his jeans.

"You're killing me," he said hoarsely.

She looked up, meeting his gaze, her smile inviting. "But what a way to go."

David ditched his jeans and briefs within seconds and led her to the bed. He kissed her, gently fisting a handful of her glorious hair so he could deepen the kiss, taking her tongue into his own mouth and experiencing a wave of arousal surge across his skin that was so intense for a second he thought he might pass out. But Annie steadied him, holding his shoulders, pressing closer, throwing back her head so he could kiss her throat, her neck, the soft skin along her shoulders. He caressed her breasts, feeling the weight of them in his hands, gently rubbing the nipples with his thumbs and feeling them stiffen beneath his touch. She moaned as David laid her back against the pillow, her beautiful hair fanned out around her. He kissed her again, deeper and longer, then he touched her as he ached to do for so long.

Foreplay had never felt so good, he thought in a kind of mindless state of pleasure. For the following hour, they kissed and touched and became acquainted with each other. There was nothing shy about Annie's touch, nothing coy about the words she whispered against his mouth and neck and chest and then lower still. She knew where to kiss, and how. She knew where to touch, when to hold, when to release. On some level, it was as though they had been lovers in another life. When he caressed her intimately she moved against him, and he watched, fascinated as her skin flushed with pleasure as she came apart in his arms, saying his name over and over.

He grabbed a condom from the unopened packet in the bedside drawer, sheathed himself, and moved over her, cradling her face within his hands, taking his weight on his forearms. David watched her for a moment, still breathing hard from her climax, seeing such pleasure in her face it tightened his chest to the point he wasn't sure he could breathe.

"Annie," he said her name on a sigh and moved between her thighs. "You feel so good."

Her hands moved to his shoulders and she pulled him closer. "You, too," she said, her eyes darkening. "You're pretty good at this."

He chuckled, loving that she could find humor alongside passion and desire. "You're not so bad yourself."

She smiled and pulled his head to her lips and kissed him, laughing delightedly against his mouth, whispering words that were meant for lovers. They kissed, they moved, they found a rhythm that was sinfully pleasurable and when release came to them both, it was sharp and sweet and wonderous and left David knowing one undeniable fact—that he had somehow, despite every intention to the contrary—spectacularly fallen head over heels in love with Annie Jamison.

Annie had been staring at the ceiling for close to half an hour, thinking about how she could drag herself out of David's bed without waking him and sneak out of the house without being seen by the kids, his grandmother and probably anyone else who resided on the place.

But since her arm was trapped beneath his and if she moved he would stir, she remained where she was, naked and still thoroughly exhausted from the almost three-hour lovemaking session they'd shared. He slept on his stomach, which was endearingly cute, and she had to stop herself from running her fingers through his hair or tracing kisses along his back and hips, or stroking the tattoo of his children's names on his shoulder.

And really, she had pretty much touched and kissed him *everywhere*. It's not like there was somewhere new for her hands and lips to roam. The sex had been amazing. She'd never experienced anything like it before. There was reverence in his touch. Gentleness alongside passion. And making love with him had only deepened the love in her heart.

Only now, of course, the regret he'd known she would have, had settled firmly in and she had one thought going through her head—*Escape*. She could see moonlight through a gap in the curtains and glanced at the clock on the bedside table. Two thirty. Right…if she snuck out now she ran the risk of waking up the entire household and the last thing the kids needed was to witness her racing from their father's bedroom like a thief in the night.

He moaned and moved unexpectedly, grasping her hand and rolling her over, pinning her beneath him. "You're awake," she said and grabbed his shoulders.

"I am," he said and teased the underside of her breast with one large hand. "You feel so lovely," he said and took the straining nipple into his mouth and laved the aching bud with his tongue.

"So, yeah," she said and arched her back as pleasure shot down her spine, holding his head between her hands as he caressed her breasts with his mouth, "you're *definitely* not a leg man."

"Told you so," he muttered against her flesh and trailed kisses upward between her breasts and up her throat until he found her lips. "But you can't blame me," he said and kissed her hotly. "Your body is amazing and should be worshipped."

When he pulled back she was breathless and panting. She met his gaze, losing herself in the greenness of his eyes. "David…"

"No," he said and gently placed a finger to her lips. "No regrets, Annie. Not when this feels so right."

It did feel right. That was the problem. "You know we need to talk about it."

He shrugged. "Maybe, but not right now. I don't want this to end."

Annie touched his jaw. "I think that's the most romantic thing I've ever heard you say."

He smiled sexily. "You don't think I'm romantic, is that it?"

"Not especially," she replied, still smiling. "You're very practical and sensible, which is why you make an excellent accountant. But romance isn't your thing. I can't imagine you raiding a flower bed to pick a bouquet or reciting a poem, can you?"

He frowned mockingly. "Guys actually do that?"

"Some," she replied. "For example, how often did you buy flowers for that woman you dated last year?"

He knew she was well aware of the other woman's name and seemed amused she didn't want to say it. "Rachel wasn't the type of woman who liked flowers."

"What type was she?"

He traced a long finger down her cheek. "What difference does it make? She was very focused on her career—which is fine—but she wasn't interested in making room for family and kids. Which is a big part of why we broke up, remember? There's no need to be jealous."

"I'm not jealous," she refuted hotly.

"Sure you are," he chuckled and kissed her again. "And since you are, without reason I might add, it's probably a good time for you to finally reconsider my proposal, don't you think?"

"Actually, I *don't* think so," she said and thought about scrambling out of bed and then considered her earlier problem about waking everyone up. "We'll talk about it when we're not…you know, in a post-sex daze."

He laughed softly, grasped both her hands and held them loosely over her head. "There's nothing *post* about right now, Annie," he said, kissing her and then proceeding to make love to her again.

It was after five thirty when Annie opened her eyes, blinked and realized the sun was about to rise and she had very little time to grab her things and leave with at least some of her dignity intact. Because as amazing as the night had been, she knew the morning would bring with it an evitable post-mortem and she wasn't in any state to start thinking about what making love with David actually meant. It was much easier to bail and think about it when she was alone and not bombarded with the familiar surroundings of the ranch and the people in it—all of whom she loved dearly.

David was still asleep, one arm flopped over his forehead, his gentle breathing the only sound in the room. She dragged herself from the bed and got dressed as quietly as she could, slipping into her shoes as she looked around for her bag, quickly realizing she'd left it in the kitchen. She tiptoed from the room, made a hasty retreat down the hall and entered the kitchen, only to find Mittie sitting at the table, a steaming cup of coffee in her hand. The older woman looked up the moment she crossed the threshold.

"Good morning," Mittie said and smiled. "Coffee?"

Annie shook her head. "Er...no, I should be going."

"Making a quick getaway?"

Heat punched her cheeks. "Something like that."

"I take it you didn't sleep in your old room last night?" Mittie asked bluntly.

Annie couldn't lie to the other woman. "Are you disappointed in me?"

"It's not my place to make judgements," Mittie replied gently.

"It's never happened before," she said, heat crawling up her neck. "I mean, David and I have never... you know..."

"I know that. It's just... Annie, I don't want to see you get hurt. I know my grandson is a good man. A little blind about some things, like most men, I suspect, but his intentions are generally honest ones. Except for when it comes to you."

Annie inhaled sharply. "You don't think he's honest with me?"

She shook her head. "I don't think he's honest with himself. I don't think he's been honest with himself about you from the very first day you started working here." Mittie smiled and sighed. "He came and spoke to me, you know, after he interviewed you. He said you were the first person he'd interviewed for the nanny position who'd asked him about Jayne. Do you remember what you asked?"

Annie nodded, remembering. "I asked if she used to sing to the children at bedtime."

"That meant a lot to him," Mittie said, "knowing you were thoughtful enough to think about such a thing. Of course, Jayne wasn't much of a singer but she used to read to Jasper a lot. She really didn't have enough time with Scarlett." She shook her head sadly. "It's funny the things you remember when someone is gone. Jayne was a lovely woman, truly, she didn't have a mean bone in her body—but I'm not sure she and my grandson would have gone the distance. Oh, they loved one another, but they never seemed to truly *need* one another." Mittie sighed heavily. "Ah, well, perhaps I'm an overly romantic fool who believes real love is when two people need one another the way we need air in our lungs or ground beneath our feet. I had that with my husband, so I think that's why I never remarried. That kind of love doesn't happen every day."

"I don't think you're overly romantic," Annie said, and smiled. "I believe in that kind of love, too."

"That's why you left, isn't it?" Mittie asked gently. "Because you love David too deeply to stay?"

She nodded, blinking away the tears in her eyes. "Yes."

"And last night?"

Annie's throat burned. "He needed someone. I was there."

Mittie touched her hand. "He does care about you, Annie."

"I know that," she said and grabbed her tote from the countertop.

"But that's not enough, is it?" Mittie ventured to ask.

Annie looked at the other woman and saw compassion and understanding in her expression.

"No, it's not enough. I want more."

And as she drove away from the ranch and headed back to the hotel, Annie realized she didn't just want more. She wanted everything.

In her heart she knew that David didn't have everything to give her. Oh, he'd marry her, because it's what his children wanted. And he'd give her a baby of her own because that's what she wanted. But his love wasn't part of the deal.

And for Annie, that was the deal breaker.

Chapter Eleven

"I'm so relieved Dad had another good night."

David half heard his sister's words. They were at the hospital on Thursday, sitting side by side in a small waiting room specifically for relatives of patients. The doctor had spoken to them at length about their father's condition and recovery. Of course he was grateful Ivan was getter better and had gone through the last forty eight hours without a stroke reoccurring. The doctor had indicated there could be some memory loss, and of course he was still struggling with the paralysis of his left side, but he was speaking much better and eating well. Ivan was lucky and they were all thankful he was on the road to recovery, even if the journey was likely to be a slow one.

But David was also completely wired and couldn't concentrate on anything other than the fact he'd spent an incredible night with Annie in his arms... and how she'd snuck off while he slept.

"Are you listening to me?" Leah complained and shoved his shoulder with her own.

David shook himself and got his thoughts quickly back to the conversation. "Uh, yeah. Sure, of course."

Leah sighed. "I think I'll need to move in with Dad for a while," she said quietly, biting her lower lip. "He lives all alone in that big house. We could hire a nurse or something, while he's doing rehab, but I'd prefer to be there in case he relapses. I'd be devastated if something happened again and one of us wasn't there for him."

"I did suggest he consider moving into the ranch for a while," David said and shrugged. "He refused."

"I know," she said and nodded. "But you know Dad, he's so stubborn about things. The best solution is for me to move in."

"He's not going to want you fussing over him."

She nodded. "I know. But I'll fuss anyway."

David knew Ivan would protest the idea of Leah moving in, but he didn't make another comment. He had enough problems without inviting more.

*The realization that he was in love with Annie had s*hocked him to the core. And it had nothing to do with her being the right person to look after his kids. He wasn't even sure how it had happened. For years he'd programmed himself to see her only as the nanny. He'd been blinding himself from the truth. But over time, he'd fallen in love—with her kindness and goodness, with her soft beauty and sweet smile. And now that he knew, David wanted to be with her and make her his own.

Except she wasn't answering his calls or texts.

He had no idea why. Of course he could speculate—that she regretted making love with him. Which was crazy because it had been incredible. Sexy and passionate and mind-blowing, but also fun and breathtakingly intimate. Everything it should be, he figured. And he certainly didn't regret it. He regretted the fact he hadn't spent the time to talk with her, to explain what he was feeling, and to ask if she was feeling the same way. To hope that she was, because the idea that she wasn't made him ache down to the soles of his feet.

"What about your job?" he asked, trying to get back to the conversation at hand.

He knew Leah liked her job, but sensed she was longing to work on her own art full-time. He'd offered to help set up her studio at Ivan's many times. But she could be stubborn, too, much like her father.

She shrugged. "I'll take some personal time and go back when Dad's on his feet."

"Or, as I've suggested before, you could quit and

turn the old shed at Dad's place into a studio and do what you really love."

"You mean become a starving artist again?" She raised both brows. "No thanks. I tried that once before and failed big time."

"*It* failed," he pointed out, "not you. And it failed because you put your faith in your ex and he turned out to be a lying SOB who couldn't be trusted and stole from you. Not your fault," he added. "There's opportunity out there, Leah, you just need to take it."

"Spoken like a typically protective big brother," she said and smiled. "Which I love you for. But I'm not ready to come out of my cave of polarizing insecurity just yet." She looked at him oddly. "Something on your mind, David? I mean, other than Dad?"

David shook his head. He didn't want to get into it with Leah. But he knew he needed to speak with Annie—and soon. "I'll check on Dad now, plus he's got a full rehab schedule today, but maybe we could meet here around dinner time. I'll bring the kids and stop by JoJo's to pick up some of that minestrone soup that dad likes."

"You're rambling," Leah said and laughed gently. "But since we're all worried about Dad and you clearly don't want to talk about what else is concerning you—which, by the way, I know is Annie—then I'll let you off the hook. I have to go home and get a few things for Dad, but I'll see you tonight." She kissed his cheek and headed off. Once she was out of sight, David returned to Ivan's room.

"You look much better today," he said when he spotted his dad sitting up in bed.

Ivan managed a lopsided smile. "Can't say the same about you."

"Girl trouble," he said and shrugged. "You know how it is."

"Haven't had girl trouble for a while," his dad said, his voice a little slurred. "Not that your mom was trouble. Best thing that ever happened to me. I got you in the deal and then Leah...luckiest man alive."

"I'm pretty sure I was the lucky one," David said, his throat thickening. "Mom was a smart woman and knew you were going to be a great father."

"I've loved every minute of being your dad, David,"

Ivan said and smiled a little. "So, have you fixed things with Annie?"

"Not exactly," he replied. "I might have made them worse."

Ivan grimaced. "You know, we all love that girl."

David nodded. "I know we do."

"Ah," Ivan said and sighed, "you've finally worked out that you're in love with her?"

"Yes."

"About time," his father said, his words slurring a little. "She's one in a million."

He nodded again. "I'm pretty sure she hates me at the moment."

Ivan laughed a little and David realized how good it was to hear the sound. "You know, your mother and I were friends for a couple of years before we got married."

"Did you always know that you were in love with her?" he asked.

"No," Ivan replied. "But we got along so well as friends, and of course she had this little boy who was delightful and over time I fell in love with you both. Now, go and sort things out with Annie…make it right… I promise you won't regret it."

David hugged his dad and left and headed directly to the O'Sullivan hotel, sending Annie a text once he reached the foyer.

Can we talk? I'm downstairs. D.

Of course, he didn't know if she was in her room. Or even if she was still staying at the hotel. Or what he was going to say when he saw her.

I love you like crazy…please marry me?

He waited a few minutes, feeling foolishly conspicuous as he stood by a huge floral arrangement in the center of the foyer. He looked around, noticing a few people he knew, and waved casually, stiffening when his cell pinged.

I'll be down in five.

Right. So, not an invitation to talk in her room, which was what he would have preferred so they could have some privacy and he could tell her how he felt. Which wasn't going to be easy. David rarely talked about his feelings. *Rarely?* More like never. Maybe that's why Jayne suited him. She was as practical as he was. Or maybe, if he looked deeper, he needed someone who was emotional and passionate and made him man up and admit to his feelings. Someone like Annie.

When she emerged from the elevator several minutes later every muscle in his body was tightly coiled. He met her halfway across the foyer. She looked sexy in black trousers, a pale green shirt, heels, and her hair up in a stylish twist. It occurred to him that she looked smart and professional and much less casual than usual.

"You look nice," he said quietly.

She pressed a hand to her hair. "I just got back from a job interview."

"A local job?" he asked, hoping that it was, hating the idea of her working in or moving to somewhere far away.

Like Texas.

"Rapid City."

Not too far away. "How did it go?"

"Good. Ah—your text said you wanted to talk?"

David nodded, discomfiture settling behind his ribs. "Feel like taking a walk?" he suggested.

She glanced down to her feet. "Not in these heels."

He motioned to the restaurant. "How about coffee?"

She agreed and minutes later they were settled at a table and had placed an order. "So, let's talk," she said and exhaled. "How's Ivan?"

"Better," David replied. "He'll be in the hospital for a few more days and has a schedule filled with rehab and therapy for the next few weeks at least, but hopefully he'll make a full recovery. Leah is going to move in with him for a while."

"I'm glad to hear he's going to be fine. How are the kids?"

David swallowed hard and rested his elbows on the table. "As much as I appreciate your concern, I didn't come here to talk about my dad or my children. I wanted to discuss this situation."

Their coffee arrived and once the waitress left, Annie spoke. "Situation?"

"Us," he replied.

"We're a *situation* now?"

"I don't know what we are," he said flatly. "You left pretty abruptly the other day."

"I didn't want the kids to see me," she said frankly and spooned a little sugar into her coffee. "It would only confuse them."

"It confused me, too," he said and met her gaze. "I thought you might have…"

"Might have what?" she prompted when his words trailed.

"Stayed," he responded. "Talked. Listened. I don't know...something."

"I didn't want to overanalyze things," she said. "I still don't."

"When we were in bed together, after we made love, I asked you to marry me," he reminded her. "Again. So...have you considered it?"

She sat back in her seat, her eyes bright, but glaring at him. "Seriously, this is what you wanted to talk about? And how?" She laughed brittlely. "You really suck at proposing, David."

"I was only trying to—"

"I know what you're trying to do," she said hotly. "You're trying to solve an equation, fix a problem, But I'm a woman, David. I'm a *person*. I deserve more than to be thought of as anyone's easy option. I want to be the only person in the world they see. I want it all—the flowers and poems and, hell, even romantic declarations from below a balcony if I can get them." She pushed the coffee aside and got to her feet. "Thank you for the...offer," she said tightly. "But, no, thank you."

She walked off and David quickly dropped a few bills on the table and raced after her. He reached her by the doorway and gently grasped her arm, turning her around.

"Annie, please listen," he said, taking a breath,

garnering his courage. "I promise you, I see you as the woman I—"

"Annie!"

A voice bellowing her name cut through his words and they both turned to face the sound. A man, carrying an overnight bag in one hand and a jacket and huge bouquet of flowers in the other, came barreling toward them. He was a big guy. Tall and broad with arms the size of tree trunks and a beaming smile. David's gut sank. It had to be the fireman.

"Byron?"

David dropped his hand immediately and watched as the guy zoomed in on her and swiftly hauled her into his arms in a hefty bear hug. He took a step back as emotions swirled in his stomach—confusion, hurt, anger—then gathered momentum. The hugging was going on for far too long. But it gave him a good opportunity to take a long look at the man embracing the woman he loved. Handsome, he supposed you'd call him, in a rugged kind of way.

It was official. He hated him.

But it didn't look like Annie hated him. In fact, it looked like quite the opposite.

Which made him madder than hell and he wanted to punch the intruder in his perfectly straight teeth.

Fight or flight—that's all he could think about. And had no illusions. Not that he'd had to hold his own in a bar brawl lately, but he'd had a few fights alongside his cousins with the O'Sullivan boys when he was at high school and generally came out without too much damage done. However, if he fought the fireman, he was pretty sure the guy would knock him out with one punch. Still, leaving wasn't an option, either.

"Hey, beautiful," the other man said now she was out of his arms. "Let me take a look at you. Wow," he said and gave an appreciative whistle. "You're even more gorgeous in person."

David's hands tingled and he fought the urge to stand in front of her like a jealous fool.

"Ah, Byron," he heard her say. "This is my...my former boss, David McCall. David." She said his name quietly, like she was wishing him to be somewhere else. "This is Byron Eckart, my..."

Future husband? Future father of her children? Future, full stop?

Her words trailed off and he didn't want to think about it, let alone shake the other man's hand. But he did, hating every moment of the interaction. And then forced himself to make polite conversation, all the while letting his hopes for a real future die inside.

Because he'd lost her, for real this time.

The thing about emotional drama, Annie discovered, is that sometimes it jumped up and bit you when you least expected it. Like now, she thought, once she'd untangled herself from Byron's Paul Bunyanesque embrace, and made the introductions. Because now she had to figure out what on earth she was going to do, and say, to a man she'd encouraged to come to Cedar River to meet her—and then, because of everything that had happened since Ivan's collapse, promptly forgotten all about.

Well, almost forgotten.

She did know he planned on visiting. But she wasn't expecting him to show up in the foyer of her hotel while she was with David. And she had no idea what David must be thinking.

Not happy, was the first thought when she met his gaze and saw his expression.

"It's nice to meet you," Byron said with a broad grin. "You're a tax attorney, right?" he asked, making the profession sound as dull as ditchwater.

"Accountant," David corrected.

"I've got one of those back home," Byron said, still grinning. "So if things work out between me and Annie, you don't need to worry about her doing her taxes in the future."

Annie could feel the tension emanating from David as the seconds ticked by and was relieved when Byron excused himself to check in.

"I know we need to talk," she said to David, moving to the side so they had some privacy. "But not now."

He didn't budge. "I'm not comfortable leaving you here with some guy you've never met."

"It's a public place," she reminded him, gesturing around at all the people. "And I'm perfectly safe here. Please go."

David stiffened. "You'd rather be with him than with me?"

"I'd rather not have this conversation," she replied.

His gaze narrowed. "Wait a minute. Were you *expecting* him?"

"Not exactly," she replied. "I mean, I knew he was coming but I—"

"You knew *when*?" he demanded. "Before or after we—"

"Before," she said quickly. "But I wasn't sure when he—"

"And it didn't occur to you to contact him and tell him not to come here? And explain that you were already—"

"Already what, David?" she demanded, cutting him off. "Taken? Hooked up? Off the market? *Engaged?* I'm not your property. I can do what I like and with whom I like."

"And you like this guy?" he asked incredulously. "Is that it?"

"Yes, David, I do Enough to marry him? I don't know," she shot back. "Maybe. He's nice. And he made the *effort* to come all this way to see me. So, I'm going to respect that effort and spend some time getting to know him. Now please leave and don't cause a scene."

David strode off without another word.

She waited until he was out of sight before concentrating on the man who was now back in front of her, and who was clearly delighted to see her and seemed even nicer in person than in all their video chats.

Once he'd checked into his own room she met him for a drink in the bar and talked about his trip, his job, his hometown and hers, and their possible future. He spoke about Texas, telling her about all the places he would take her if she visited. Annie realized she should have been jumping for joy because a really nice man—and one who clearly liked her— had traveled a very long way to meet up and hopefully kindle their romance. But she wasn't jumping. She wasn't anything other than completely miserable. And confused.

This is what you wanted, remember?

Someone romantic. Okay, he ticked the box, as over drinks he gave her the flowers he'd brought, and a lovely book of poetry he thought she would like. And he'd written a sweet message on the inside page.

Someone insightful—because he immediately asked her if she was okay with him being there, assured her there was no pressure and they could get to know one another at whatever pace she wanted.

Someone who *saw* her—which he obviously did as he told her several times how beautiful she was.

Someone who made her laugh—he ticked that

box too, because he was funny and charming and made her smile.

Yes, Byron was perfect. Except for one important fact.

He wasn't David McCall.

And it didn't feel as though David was going to be purged from her heart any time soon.

Only, Annie knew she owed it to Byron to make an effort. He was friendly and talkative and utterly unthreatening. She *should* have been falling in love with him with each passing second.

But she wasn't.

"Can I take you to dinner tonight?" he asked as they crossed the foyer to the elevator.

"Sure. The restaurant here is really good."

"I actually feel like pizza," he said cheerfully. "Can we get that here? Or can you suggest somewhere else?"

She told him about JoJo's and made arrangements to meet him back in the foyer at six o'clock.

She headed to her room and called her sister, explaining that Byron had shown up—leaving out any mention of David.

"And is he everything you hoped for?" Tess asked.

"Yes," she replied. "He's very nice. And he seems to like me."

"Of course he likes you," Tess assured her. "You're amazing. Have a good time and stay safe. Text me when you get back to your room."

She dressed in jeans, a bright red shirt and boots and met Byron in the foyer at exactly six o'clock. They walked the half block to JoJo's and quickly got a booth. They ordered pizza with extra pineapple and were just about to tuck in to their first slices when she saw David walk into the restaurant, holding Scarlett in his arms while Jasper walked by his side.

Her heart rolled over at the sight of them and a deep-rooted longing made every part of her ache. Her eyes burned and she blinked, pushing back the tears that threatened to roll down her cheeks.

It was never meant to be this hard.

"Everything okay?"

Byron's query forced her to nod and avert her gaze, but not before she saw David glance in her direction. And his look almost ended her.

Annie saw him collect a takeout order and then leave quickly and was glad the kids hadn't noticed her.

She was back at the hotel an hour later and said good-night to Byron. He kissed her lightly, and although she sensed he wanted more, he didn't try to persuade his way into her room or her bed. It was a nice, gentle kiss. With zero impact.

And, she suspected they both knew it.

Over breakfast the following morning, Annie told Byron she didn't have the feelings for him that either of them had hoped for. He took it well, better than she expected or deserved. And he assured her there were no hard feelings. She knew he was disappointed and obviously a little hurt, but he was a gentleman and suggested they remain friends.

"Is there someone else?" Byron asked and smiled.

She shrugged. "There's the *idea* of someone else."

"Your ex boss?" he queried. "The one I met yesterday? I'm guessing it's him."

She nodded, her chest tightening. "How did you know?"

"You talk about him a lot."

She was startled by his words. "I don't remember doing that."

"You talked about the kids a lot. He was part of the package. I figured it out pretty early on. You've loved him a long time, right?"

She nodded. "You could say that. I'm sorry, I didn't mean to lead you on, or make you think I was ready for a relationship."

He sat back in his seat. "I think you are ready... just not with me." He smiled at her—a little sadly, she thought. "But maybe, when you're ready...we could still be friends?"

She nodded. "I'd like that."

He got to his feet and held out his hand. "Goodbye, Annie."

She shook his hand, relieved that he didn't try to kiss her again. And when he left the hotel a short time later, Annie didn't have one spark of regret.

Midmorning she got a call from David and ignored it. Followed by a text. Which she also ignored. She didn't want to talk. She didn't want to see him.

She did, however, call her sister.

"I'm tired of living at the hotel. Can I come and stay with you for a while?"

"Of course," Tess declared. "And I insist you come now."

She didn't need any more encouragement and quickly packed her bags, settled her bill at the front desk, and left for the Triple C. Her sister greeted her with smiles and hugs and so much love Annie burst into tears.

"Oh, Tess," she said as her sister hugged her shoulders and they walked up to the house. "I don't know what to do." She explained quickly about Byron.

"I guess you can't force love, eh?" Tess said gently as they settled in the guest room upstairs.

"Nope. Byron is a nice guy, really nice. And he took it like a champion. He asked if we could be friends and I thought it might be nice to have a male friend—I've not had one of those since college. I mean, the only other guy I hang out with is Mitch and he's my brother-in-law, so he doesn't count. I guess Jake and the rest of Mitch's brothers are all kind of in the friend zone."

"And David?"

"I'm not sure *friend-zone* fits anymore," she said and colored hotly as she sat on the edge of the bed.

Tess's eyes widened into saucers. "You had sex with him?"

She nodded. "Don't be mad at me," she said quickly. "It was after Ivan was rushed to hospital. You know how I went and watched the kids and then David came home and we… I don't know…it was stupid, but I couldn't help myself."

Her sister nodded. "Don't be silly—I'm not mad. I'm concerned that you're going to get your heart broken."

"Too late."

"So, he just what?" Tess asked. "Used you for comfort sex because his father was sick?"

"No, it wasn't like that," Annie said in defense, hating that her sister thought so badly of him. "He actually proposed again."

"And?"

"Well, he's done that before and this time was just as bad."

Tess didn't bother to hide her concern. "Hang on. David asked you to marry him again, and you refused again?"

She nodded. "He thinks it would be a great idea because the kids love me and everything would stay the same. I could go back to living at the ranch, have a baby and the world would turn as per usual. It's quite the offer, don't you think?"

Tess hugged her. "Oh, honey, I'm sorry."

Annie sighed. "The thing is, as crazy as it seems, I *do* want to marry David. I want to be with the kids.

And I want to have a baby with him. But I can't do it without…without…"

"His love?"

She nodded. "He's pretty much made it clear that's not on the table. Companionship and friendship and sex…that's the offer."

"He actually said that?"

"No," she replied. "But I *know* David. I know how he thinks. I know how he tends to over-think things. I want a partnership and I want the father of my children to need me as I need him. I want the kind of love you have with Mitch, or Abby has with Jake, or like our parents have."

"And you're sure you can't have that with David?" Tess asked.

"He's asked me to marry him more than once in the past couple of weeks," she admitted. "And on none of those occasions did he mention anything about how he really feels—only about how sensible the arrangement would be." She shook her head. "Maybe he just can't love anyone anymore. Not after…" She took a deep, shuddering breath. "Not after Jayne."

Of course, she didn't quite believe that. She knew David had a great capacity for love. She'd witnessed that love firsthand when he was with his children, and his whole family. Even when he was married to Jayne, on the few occasions she had seen them together, she remembered him being attentive and loving.

Maybe it's just me? Perhaps I'm not the kind of woman that a man falls crazy in love with.

The truth was, she'd had very little romance in her life and never had a man say he loved her. The relationships she'd had in college were too young, too brief, to really be about that kind of emotion. She hiccupped back a sob, for a moment thinking about how it made her feel, as though she was unlovable and dull. And then she scolded herself for being ridiculous. Just because David hadn't fallen madly in love with her, it didn't mean someone else wouldn't. The only thing was, she didn't want anyone else.

"I need to forget about this and think about what I can control," she announced, determined to put it all behind her. She quickly told her sister about the interview in Rapid City. "It went well, I think. It's only part-time, but with my savings I can manage with that for a while. And another woman at a job I interviewed for last week wants to bring me back again for a second interview, so we'll see."

"Well, I insist you live here with us," Tess said firmly. "Until you work out where you want to be. And don't say no," her sister added when Annie held up a hand. "Mitch will insist, too."

Annie nodded agreeably. "I don't quite know what's come over me. I never used to be sentimental and sappy and... I don't know," she said and sighed, "*pathetic*."

"You're not pathetic," Tess said firmly and sat beside her. "You have a broken heart. Remember how I was an emotional wreck when I came back to Cedar River last year—pregnant after a one-night stand with my ex-husband, who I had convinced myself had no feelings left for me whatsoever? You were my rock back then, Annie. Let me be your rock now. That's what family does for each other."

Tears returned to her eyes and she blinked quickly. She needed a rock. She needed safe harbor.

She needed David.

And he, she suspected, needed her. Making love with him had cemented in her heart what she knew—that he was as vulnerable as she, and as alone. The intimacy they'd shared was more real than any she'd shared before—the words he whispered against her skin were from a place deep down, where secrets and fears lay.

I'm so tired of loss...

There had been real pain in those words and she understood. But she wasn't going to force his hand. If he wanted her, he needed to come for her with his heart exposed, and not hiding behind words about marrying her because it was good for the kids. It would be, she was sure. But it wasn't enough. No, she wanted it all.

All or nothing.

Chapter Twelve

In all his life, David had never felt more emotionally out of control. Even when Jayne and his mother had died, he'd been able to focus, to put all his energy into raising the kids, to his job, and to helping Ivan and Leah work through their grief.

But this was different.

This was pain on a whole new level.

Seeing her at JoJo's with the fireman had broken him up inside. She was on a date. Enjoying herself. Talking, laughing. Sharing her life with another man.

He called Annie Friday morning, longing to hear her voice, to talk, but it went to her voice mail. He texted and she didn't respond. It galvanized him into

action and on Friday afternoon he went back to the
O'Sullivan hotel, only to discover she'd checked out.
Gone. Run off with her fireman.

Man, I'm an idiot.

Pain set in, lodging in his chest like a knife. And
jealousy – the unrelenting kind that made his gut
churn and his heart ache behind his ribs.

He hurt all over. He should have fought harder,
and now he'd lost her because he was unable to
admit what he was feeling.

He drove home and was faced with the news from
the new nanny that she was resigning. She liked the
job and the kids were lovely, but she missed looking
after her own grandchildren full-time too much and
was moving in with her daughter's family.

Right. He had no clue what to do. Close down the
practice for a couple of weeks until he found a new
nanny? Since Mittie was leaving for her Alaskan trip
soon, Leah was looking after their dad, and Tess had
a young baby, he was all out of child-sitting options.

"Did you at least insist on a couple of weeks' notice?" Leah asked early on Saturday morning. She'd
dropped by the ranch to go through the contractors
quote she had done for getting a ramp installed at
Ivan's so he could easily maneuver his wheelchair
into the house. The kids were still in bed and he was
on to his second cup of coffee.

David shrugged. "She said she'd stay a week.
But honestly, I don't want someone here who wants
to be somewhere else. The kids would pick up on it

and they're feeling fragile enough at the moment, I don't want an unwilling nanny added to the mix," he said wearily.

He'd had a crappy night's sleep, spending most of the night staring at the ceiling and imagining he could still pick up the traces of Annie's perfume in the bed sheets. Which was ridiculous, since the linen had been changed many times since then. But he'd be damned if he didn't feel as though he inhaled the scent every time he sucked in a breath.

"I'll help out of course, at least when I can. What are you going to do?"

"Get a new nanny."

"And...what else?"

He shrugged again. "I have no idea."

"Daddy?"

David turned in his seat and spotted his son in the doorway. "Yes, buddy?"

"Scarlett and I don't want a new nanny," he said matter-of-factly. "We just want Annie."

He exhaled heavily. "I know you do, but Annie isn't—"

"Annie loves us," Jasper said simply. "And we love her. Why don't we tell her that, so she'll come home?"

David stared at his son and an odd sensation formed in the center of his chest. He wasn't sure how he could tell his son the truth—that Annie had left town. Of course, he didn't have any real proof. But since she wasn't at the hotel it was fair to assume she'd simply gone off-grid with her fireman for a while—an image he really didn't want to think about.

He considered asking Leah to track her down, then changed his mind because the notion was too humiliating. And he didn't want any more of his sister's advice. Then he thought about calling Tess, and instead decided to take the kids to the Triple C for a visit and as a way of exorcising the demons raging through his system. He'd get straight talking from Mitch, which was what he needed. He had to forget about any fantasy he had regarding Annie—she'd made her choice when she sent him away.

It was midmorning when he pulled up at the Culhane ranch. The kids sped up the pathway, headed straight for the house and David quickly followed. Mitch greeted him on the front porch with a handshake and they walked inside.

"You look like crap," Mitch said bluntly. "Not sleeping?"

"Not much."

Mitch shook his head. "You screwed up, huh?"

David ignored the dig. "How's my godson?" he asked as they walked down the hall and made their way to the kitchen.

"Perfect in every way," Mitch said of his son. "I never imagined I'd enjoy fatherhood so much."

David nodded. "Brings life into perspective."

"It certainly does. As does being married to the

woman I love. I feel like the luckiest man on the planet."

"That must be a nice feeling."

"It is," Mitch replied. "I'm very grateful that Tess forgave me for being an idiot and took me back."

"I miss being married," David admitted. "As much as I enjoy your company, I miss having a woman to talk to, one who isn't my sister or grandmother or cousin. After Jayne died, I never imagined I'd feel something for someone else...but I did... I do," he said and shrugged. "Too late to wonder what might have happened."

"Too late?" Mitch inquired and grabbed a couple of sodas from the refrigerator as the kids sat up at the countertop. "Why is that?"

"Annie's gone," he said quietly so the kids couldn't hear. "She took off with her fireman."

Mitch's brows shot up. "She did?"

He nodded. "She checked out of the hotel yesterday and won't return my calls."

"Did you give her a reason not to?"

He sighed. "Admittedly, I've behaved stupidly about some things. But I can't believe she ran off with some guy she just met. It's so unlike her."

"You think you know Annie pretty well, don't you?"

David frowned. "Well...yeah."

Mitch laughed and shook his head. "Be back in a minute," he said and left the room.

David got to his feet and moved to the counter,

listening to Jasper talk about his plans for the day when he heard movement from the door. He spun and then reeled back in surprise. Annie stood in the door, in jeans, T-shirt and cowboy boots.

He said her name and frowned. "What are you doing?"

She pointed to her cowboy boots. "Going riding on Star."

"I mean what are you doing here?" he demanded.

"I live here," she said and held out a hand for each of the kids as they jumped off their stools and raced toward her. "Well, for the moment."

"Annie, Annie!" Jasper chanted happily and then proceeded to tell her about his week at school, while Scarlett begged to be picked up and cuddled before talking about the new dress her aunt had bought her. "Our new nanny isn't going to look after us anymore," Jasper announced.

David shrugged when Annie shot him a curious look. "She quit. Happening to me a lot lately."

A smile touched the corners of her lips. "I can't imagine why."

"We miss you," Jasper said and looked at David. "Don't we, Dad?"

David didn't respond, still reeling from the fact she was at the ranch and not on the run with her fireman boyfriend. "You live *here*?" he echoed blankly.

She nodded. "I'm staying for a while."

"I thought you'd…"

His words trailed off and she made an irritated face. "You thought I'd what?"

"Gone to Texas," he admitted. "Left town."

Tess and Mitch suddenly appeared in the door. "Ah—how about you guys take this conversation into the living room and Mitch and I will watch the kids, okay?" Tess suggested and quickly gathered the children together. "Go on, off you go."

Annie was gone in a second and he followed without thinking. When they reached the living room she stopped by the fireplace and swiveled, facing him with her hands on her hips.

"You thought I'd left town with Byron?" she asked

Discomfiture crept up his neck. "He did have his arms around you the last time we were together."

"He was saying hello," she defended. "That's all."

"You said you liked him," he reminded her. "And you told me to leave so you could be alone with him, remember?"

"I was mad at you for your dumb marriage proposal," she said and huffed. "I'm *still* mad at you," she said and flapped her hands. "But that doesn't mean I would run off with a man I only just met in person for the first time."

"I didn't know what to think," he offered.

She made an impatient sound. "Oh, I'm pretty sure you did…and still do. What would you like to know, David? The gritty details? Like, did I kiss him? Did I let him touch me? Did I let him put his hand up my dress in the parking lot? Did I touch him back? Did I sleep with him?"

David's gut plummeted. "Annie, I didn't think—"

"Rest assured," she shot back. "I make it my business *not* to have sex with two different men in the same week."

Shame pressed down on his shoulders. Because that's what he'd been imagining. And it had been killing him. "I'm sorry. I didn't mean to suggest you were—"

"What?" she demanded. "Easy? I'm not. Believe me, jumping into your bed was an aberration on my part."

He didn't like how that sounded. Like she regretted being with him. "I would never disrespect you like that, Annie." David said and inhaled heavily. "So, where is he now? Is he here, too?"

"He's gone," she said hotly.

"Gone where?"

"Home," she replied. "Texas. He left yesterday."

The acid in his gut dispersed a little. "What does that mean?"

"It means he's gone."

"You got rid of him?"

"He left. Byron and I are not a thing."

David met her gaze as relief filled his chest. And love. "I'm glad to hear it."

"I don't know why," she said and crossed her arms. "It has nothing to do with you."

He stepped close. "I reckon it has everything to do with me."

"Wow. That's pretty conceited, David," she said softly, her voice wavering.

"At times I guess I can be," he said and stood in front of her, folding his own arms the way she was. "But I do love you, Annie."

He wasn't sure what he expected by his declaration. Perhaps some indication that she felt the same. At least, that's what he was hoping for. With some luck, she'd see they were meant for one another and finally agree to marry him.

"No, you don't," she refuted, her voice thick with emotion. "You're only saying that to get what you want."

"And what do you think that is?"

"I'm not prepared to keep going over this same old issue, David. Not until you make an effort to understand what I'm saying."

He shrugged, feeling a little helpless, and then a little irritated. "I just said that I loved you."

"I *love* my favorite pink sneakers," she said quickly. "That doesn't mean I'd marry them."

She left the room, headed down the hall and David heard the front door open, then close loudly. He remained where he was and exhaled, deciding which direction to go when his cousin appeared in the doorway.

"You really don't know much about women, do you?" Mitch said and laughed.

David scowled. "Maybe not. But I don't need lectures." He sighed. "Although, maybe I could use a little advice. Got any?"

"If you're in love with her, tell her."

"I just tried," he said and shrugged. "She didn't believe me."

"Try again," Mitch said and laughed. "Unless you don't think she's worth it."

"Of course I do," he said and ran a frustrated hand through his hair. "I'm in love with Annie, okay. I love her so much it's making me crazy. But she's not listening. She hasn't listened to me for weeks. In fact, I don't think she's heard a word I've said since she gave me her resignation."

"Perhaps they're not the words she needs to hear."

David glanced to the left of his cousin and spotted Tess regarding him with both brows up.

"*Marry me* isn't enough?" he remarked cynically.

"It's the how, not the what," Tess replied. "You might start by asking her why she gave you that resignation in the first place."

"I did ask her and she told me why," he said impatiently and then smiled when the kids popped around the corner and came into the room. "She wants to get married and have children. And maybe not with that muscle-bound fireman, but someone else will come along and win her over."

"If you believe that, then you aren't the smart guy I always pegged you for," Tess said. "It was never about Byron. Or anyone else. It was *always* about you."

He stared at Tess as if she'd grown a second head. "What... I don't understand...what does that mean?"

"It means, *think*, David...think long and hard about why Annie would leave two kids she adores like they're her own."

He stared at Tess, rocking back on his heels. "Whatever you think is going on here, I'm pretty sure that Annie doesn't...you know...she doesn't love me like that."

"Yes, she does, Dad."

They all looked toward Jasper, who had spoken the words. His son was standing in the center of the living room, watching them in turn.

"Buddy, I don't—"

"Annie told me," he announced. "And Annie doesn't lie."

David swallowed hard, looked at his kids and then his cousin and his wife. Jasper was right. Annie didn't lie. Annie always told the truth. Since she'd entered his life she'd been the voice of reason. His conscience. The one opinion he valued above all others.

You might start by asking her why she gave you that resignation in the first place...

And right then he realized he'd asked that question countless times...but never really *listened* to her response. He'd never read between the lines. He had, he realized now, been insensitive and thoughtless from the moment she'd handed him her resignation. Particularly when he offered her marriage. Not even his love. Just a marriage. A union to keep his family together.

What he didn't tell her was that he was terrified of living his life without her in it. Or that not seeing her every day was torture. Or how making love with her was the most physically and emotionally intimate experience of his life and that since then, his nights had been lonely and empty.

David looked at Tess, his chest so tight he could barely breathe, and suddenly, he knew. "My God... I can't believe it... I've been so blind."

Tess smiled and then clapped softly. "Bravo. You *are* the smart guy I always pegged you for. Now," she said and stood aside. "Go out there and *unbreak* my sister's heart."

David inhaled and smiled. "I will, but first, can you call your parents in Wyoming?"

Tess looked at him oddly. "What for?"

"Because I want to ask Ian Jamison for permission to marry his daughter."

Annie grabbed a stiff brush and began grooming Star with long methodical strokes. Grooming her horse always relaxed her and she needed relaxing— big time. If only her brain would comply and stop thinking about David and his thoughtless, hurtful, meaningless, impossibly inappropriate declaration of love. It was a low act. And if she had any sense, she would forget all about it.

He didn't love her. He couldn't possibly.

Once she was done grooming, she went to grab the hay net, deciding she wasn't in the mood to go riding. The net was empty, as was the drum that usually contained a hay bale. She looked up to the hay loft and sighed, thinking she probably could get one of the ranch hands to throw down a bale. Instead, she left Star tied up in his stall and climbed the wide ladder to the loft. The scent of sweet hay shot up her nose and she sneezed a couple of times, then grabbed one of the bales by the twine and tossed it down.

"Do you need some help?"

She looked down and spotted David near Star's stall. Standing by the door, in jeans, white shirt and cowboy boots, his glasses making him look ridiculously sexy, and carrying a bunch of flowers she realized was lavender he must have just picked on his way to the barn, her heart fluttered foolishly.

"No thanks," she said and moved to put her heel on the ladder.

"Stay up there, will you?"

She glared down. "What?"

"Stay up there for a moment," he said again and stood in the center of the barn. "I'd like to talk to you."

Annie propped her hands on her hips. "With me up here and you down there?"

"It's your balcony," he said simply.

"My what?"

"You said you wanted romantic gestures from below a balcony. And flowers," he added, and held out the lavender, roots dropping dirt onto his hair. "Remember?"

"I think I was being ironic when I said that," she observed, trying to ignore her still fluttering heart. "You know, making a point."

"Your point was taken. I could try reciting a sonnet."

She bit back a smile. "That looks like lavender from Tess's garden."

"Because it is," he replied. "It's the best I could do on short notice."

"I have no idea what you're doing, David."

He exhaled heavily, looking up. "Firstly, making amends."

"For what?"

"For thinking that you had run off with... Byron."

It was the first time she'd heard him use the other man's name. "Is that an apology?"

He nodded. "Yes."

"Apology accepted."

"Put my stupid accusation down to the fact that the very idea of you being with him made me crazy."

"You were jealous?"

He nodded. "Absolutely."

"Okay, you've made your point."

He took a breath. "Now I'd like to ask you a question...and I would like you to tell me the truth."

She stiffened. "Sure."

"Do you believe I am a man of integrity?" he asked, surprising her.

"What?"

"Do you think I'm honest and trustworthy?"

Annie had no idea where the conversation was going, but she nodded. "Of course I do."

He sighed, looking relieved. "Good…so, let's just park that for a moment. I'd like to ask you another question."

She hesitated, thinking she should get down the ladder and meet him on level ground. But she was curious and remained where she was. "Go ahead."

"You care about my children, correct?"

"You know I do."

"And they care about you, right? They regularly tell you how much you mean to them?"

She nodded. "I don't see what—"

"And my grandmother," he said, cutting her off. "She cares about you, too. She thinks you've hung the moon and tells you as much whenever she gets a chance, yes?"

"Ah…yes," she replied, thinking about how Mittie was very forthcoming with her affection and that she adored the older woman. "I don't see how this is—"

"Then there's my sister, who clearly loves you as a friend and holds you in high regard. I suspect the feeling is mutual?"

"Very much so."

"And of course, then there's my dad, who calls you an angel…would that be an exaggeration?"

She smiled, still not knowing where this was going. "No, Ivan is very sweet."

He took a second, inhaling, looking at her with his penetrating gaze. "So, we've established that my kids, my grandmother, my sister and my stepdad all care about you…love you, in fact. And you care deeply about them in return, correct?"

She nodded. "Correct."

"And when they tell you how they feel, you believe them?'

"Well…yes."

He nodded, dropping his hands to his sides, and a few lavender buds landed on the barn floor. "All right, so I'd like to go back to my earlier question when I asked you if you though I had integrity and could be trusted."

"I don't see the point in you—"

"My point," he said quietly, "is that you say you trust me. You say you think I'm honest and trustworthy. And yet," he said, pausing for a moment, "you clearly *don't* trust me."

"Of course I do. You know—"

"I know that when my kids, my grandmother, my sister and my dad tell you how they feel, you believe them." He looked at her and she got lost in his eyes. "But earlier, when I told you I loved you, you didn't believe me. Why is that?"

Annie sucked in a sharp breath. What could she say? That she was scared of believing him?

"Because I—"

"Because you think I have an agenda?" he queried, his voice breaking a little. "The only agenda I have is wanting to be with the woman who loves my children as much as I do. The woman who came into my life four years ago and helped heal my grief. Who healed my kids, my sister, my grandmother, my step-dad. The woman who made me *want* to feel again."

Annie stared at him, transfixed by the vulnerability in his words. "But you've never said anything," she reminded him, "in all the years we've know one another."

He sighed and nodded and moved to the bottom of the ladder. "Would you come down here please?"

Annie slowly made her way down the ladder. When she reached the ground he held out the flowers and she took them with a shaky hand. She inhaled the sweet scent and swallowed hard, meeting his green-eyed gaze.

"David…"

He reached out and pushed a lock of hair behind her ear. "When you first came to work for me, I was so relieved that finally I had someone who my children could trust and rely on. They bonded with you so quickly and I think I placed you inside a bubble because anything else would have been completely inappropriate." He sighed, touching her cheek. "For a long time after Jayne died, I wasn't in any sort of headspace to do anything other than raise my kids. I couldn't think about moving on with someone. And by the time I was, you and I had settled into our working relationship that made anything else impossible. And even if it hadn't been, I was too blind to see what and who was in front of me."

"What was that?" she asked softly.

"An angel," he said simply. "A healer. It occurred to me, only recently, that somehow, while we became friends and you became part of my family, while everyone else was working out how incredible you are, I was actually falling for you and didn't know it." He shrugged, cupping her cheek gently. "Stupid, huh."

"And now?" she asked, allowing happiness to seep through her.

"Now I know I am completely in love with you, Annie."

She shuddered, opening her heart, knowing now was the time to tell him how she felt. "I love you too, David."

He moved closer, putting his hand gently around her nape. "That's why you resigned? You told me once you'd been in love and he didn't love you back...you were talking about me...about us?"

She nodded. "I couldn't stay... I knew if I did, I'd never get over you."

"Promise me you won't," he said teasingly. "Get over me, I mean. I couldn't bear to lose you, Annie.

I want to spend the rest of my life with you. I want to grow old with you. I want my children to be your children. I want your face to be the last thing I see before I go to sleep at night, and the first thing I see when I wake up each morning. I want to hear your laughter in every room. I want to kiss you and make love to you. I want to marry you, if you'll have me."

Tears spilled down her cheeks. They were the most romantic words she had ever heard. "You *are* a poet," she whispered, loving him so much in that moment she thought she might burst. "And I'd love to marry you, David."

He kissed her, long and deep and sweet and Annie sighed against his mouth. "Do you know when I started to realize I was in love with you?" he murmured against her lips.

Annie gripped his shoulders. "When?"

"At the cottage that day...you know, after you resigned and we were stuck there because of the rain. It was as though the world tilted on some kind of altered axis and suddenly I was looking at you differently...perhaps really seeing you for the first time."

"As a woman, you mean?" she scolded teasingly.

"Don't be mad at me," he begged, kissing her neck. "I was trying to take the high ground by keeping you in the can't-touch category. And then I kissed you that first time and I was a goner."

Annie smiled against his mouth. "I love it when you kiss me."

"I intend to kiss you every day for the rest of my

life," he said and held her close. "When will you marry me?"

"Whenever you want."

"Soon," he said quickly. "And… I would love to have a baby with you, Annie. Maybe two."

"Or three?" she suggested, laughing.

"As many as you want, sweetheart," he said gently and wiped the tears from her cheek. "And now we should probably go back to the house and tell everyone that we're getting married. You know the kids are going to be over the moon. I did promise your sister I'd come out here and unbreak your heart."

"Mission accomplished," she said and pressed closer.

Annie looked at him, her heart filled with love and hope and happiness.

Her life had just been made, and that was the best feeling ever.

Epilogue

Four Weeks Later

"You know," Leah said as she fluffed the ivory tulle around the skirt of Annie's gown, "this really is the most stunning dress."

Annie glanced at her reflection in the long mirror, taking in the beauty of the long ivory satin gown; with its off-the-shoulder style and princess line bodice, it was incredibly flattering. She smiled, looking at her soon-to-be sister-in-law. "I know. I feel stunning wearing it."

Tess came around to face her, holding a hairpin encrusted with tiny pearls. "Mom asked if you wanted to wear this—she wore it when she married your dad…that was the day we became sisters."

Annie's eyes filled with moisture and Leah grabbed a linen handkerchief she had tucked in her purse. "No tears," she chided gently. "Or I'll have to redo your makeup."

Annie blinked and took a steadying breath. "I can't help it. I'm so happy and it's all a little overwhelming."

It had, in fact, been something of a whirlwind since she'd accepted David's proposal. They'd quickly gone engagement-and-wedding-ring shopping, taking the kids with them, who were joyously happy about the prospect of them marrying. She got a part time admin job at the Cedar River police station, working two days a week during school hours. Two days after his proposal she moved back into the ranch and they had begun planning their wedding. Small by some standards, but as romantic as Annie had ever dreamed about. They'd decided to stick with Culhane tradition and get married at the Triple C, by the orchard and underneath a huge white tent, with a local band playing their favorite songs. Mitch was standing up as best man, Tess was her matron of honor and Leah, and Ellie, were bridesmaids. Scarlett was as cute as a button in her flower-girl dress and Jasper was the ring bearer. Her father was giving her away and when he stepped through the door a few minutes later, her bridesmaids disappeared and left her alone with her parent for a moment.

"You look beautiful," Ian Jamison said and hugged her gently. "Your mom would have been so proud of the woman you have become. You know, I never really believed there would ever be a man good enough for you. But I like David," he added and smiled.

"Thanks, Dad. I like him, too," she said and chuckled.

"He called me and your stepmom, you know, and asked for your hand," her dad said and grinned, tears plumping at the corners of his eyes. "He said you were the air in his lungs and the ground beneath his feet. It was all I had to hear to know he was worthy and would look after my baby girl."

Annie's eyes filled with moisture. "We took the long road to get here...but it was worth it."

Her dad hugged her gently and took her arm just as Suzanne Jamison came through the door. "It's time."

Annie nodded and walked to the door with her father, embracing her stepmother before they left the room. Tess was standing outside the room, while Ellie, Leah and Scarlett were at the bottom of the stairway and she couldn't help the beaming smile when she spotted them waiting for her.

She waited while Tess fiddled with her veil, kissed her cheek and then went on ahead. She heard music from the band playing and then the song shifted to the one she'd chosen to walk down the aisle to—a sweet, country song that was almost the storybook of her relationship with David.

They headed down the steps, then around the house and Annie held on to her father as the altar came into view. Leah and Ellie walked on ahead, meeting their groomsmen—two of Mitch's brothers, Jake and Grant, and Scarlett quickly followed, dropping petals from a basket as she wandered up the aisle. Tess moved forward and walked alone, and then Annie and her father began the steady march. She spotted David and her heart rolled over. He looked so handsome in a gray suit, ivory shirt and bolo tie. Jasper stood in front of him, wearing an identical suit, and holding a small cushion, a beaming smile on his face.

Annie met David's gaze, seeing the love he had for her in his eyes. There was no barrier, no wall up, no hesitation—just an open and sincere expression and no hint of the closed-off man she'd once believed him to be. Annie had no doubt of David's love for her and she knew he felt the same. Being in love had solidified the friendship they shared. It was a connection that had been there from the very beginning. It was why they could talk, could argue, could easily finish one another's sentences, often without realizing they were doing it. And it was why they had fallen in love. When they reached the altar, her dad released her arm and she stepped forward, taking David's hand.

"Hey there, sweetheart," he said softly.

Annie met his gaze. "Hi. Did I keep you waiting?"

He smiled. "You're right on time."

Jasper and Scarlett moved in between them, David gently released her and then they both grasped a hand of each child. The moment was achingly sweet and exactly how it should be—because they were a family.

"Are we ready to begin?" the minister asked.

Annie's eyes didn't leave David's. "You bet."

She sighed and relaxed, falling in love with David just a little bit more as she became his wife.

David had been married for exactly two hours and three minutes when he finally managed to get some alone time with his bride. Well, if you could count being at the long table, with the bridal party stretched out along each end, the music playing in the background and the kids coming up to them every few minutes to ask when they were going to cut the cake. Chocolate, of course, because his wife didn't like fruitcake.

"Have I told you how beautiful you look?" he asked and looped one arm around her, settling his hand against her shoulder.

She swayed against him, the scent of her reaching him deep down. "Several times," she replied. "Although I don't mind hearing it. I mean, how many times am I going to get the opportunity to wear a dress like this?" she teased.

David touched her cheek. "Only once, my love. Even if it means I have to fight every fireman that comes to town."

She laughed softly. "Poor Byron...he really is a nice man."

David made a grumpy face for second. "Mmm... real sweet."

"You're still jealous?" she teased again.

"Absolutely," he replied and raised her hand to his mouth before kissing her knuckles. "You know, it occurred to me that in all the time we've known one another, we've never danced."

"You have two left feet and don't like dancing," she reminded him. "And I thought we agreed we wouldn't do the 'first dance' thing."

David shrugged. "I'm turning over a new leaf and trying new things. And I know you want to."

"Even if I want to boot scoot?"

He grimaced. "Even then."

She touched his face gently. "Tell you what, I'll settle for one of those really slow, swaying against each other kind of dances."

"That actually sounds pretty good," he said and got to his feet, holding out his hand. She took it immediately and David led her to the dance floor. He motioned to the band and suddenly the music changed tempo.

Annie looked at him as the dance floor cleared and the George Strait classic *I Cross My Heart* began.

"You arranged this?" she asked and pressed her face into his neck.

He knew they were being observed, but David was oblivious to the people around them. In that moment, he only saw Annie. "You deserve to have every dream you've had realized, sweetheart. Even if that's dancing with your two-left-footed husband."

She laughed delightedly. "You can't be that bad?"

"Wanna bet?" he said and grinned.

He was, he figured, but Annie didn't seem to care. Neither did the kids when they came up and joined them on the dance floor. It was, he thought, one of those perfect moments. With plenty more to come. As he danced with his wife and children, he silently thanked Jayne, his mom and dad, and everyone who had moved through his life over the years. Because of them, he was the man Annie had chosen to trust and love and that was the greatest gift on earth.

And one he would treasure every day of his life.

* * * * *

Look for Leah's story,

The Secret Between Them

the next installment in
The Culhanes of Cedar River,
Helen Lacey's miniseries for

Harlequin Special Edition.

On sale June 2020, wherever Harlequin books
and ebooks are sold.

SPECIAL EXCERPT FROM

⬡ HARLEQUIN
SPECIAL EDITION

*When Laurel Hudson is found—alive but with
amnesia—no one is more relieved than Adam Fortune.
He will do whatever it takes to reunite mother and son,
even if it means a road trip in extremely close quarters.
Will the long journey home remind Laurel how much
they truly share?*

*Read on for a sneak preview of the final book in
The Fortunes of Texas: Rambling Rose continuity,*
The Texan's Baby Bombshell *by Allison Leigh.*

He'd been falling for her from the very beginning. But
that kiss had sealed the deal for him.

Now that glossy oak-barrel hair slid over her shoulder
as Laurel's head turned and she looked his way.

His step faltered.

Her eyes were the same stunning shade of blue they'd
always been. Her perfectly heart-shaped face was pale
and delicate looking even without the pink scar on her
forehead between her eyebrows.

Her eyebrows pulled together as their eyes met.

Remember me.

Remember us.

The words—unwanted and unexpected—pulsed
through him, drowning out the splitting headache and the
aching back and the impatience, the relief and the pain.

Then she blinked those incredible eyes of hers and he realized there was a flush on her cheeks and she was chewing at the corner of her lips. In contrast to her delicate features, her lips were just as full and pouty as they'd always been.

Kissing them had been an adventure in and of itself.

He pushed the pointless memory out of his head and then had to shove his hands in the pockets of his jeans because they were actually shaking.

"Hi." Puny first word to say to the woman who'd made a wreck out of him.

Still seated, she looked up at him. "Hi." She sounded breathless. "It's…it's Adam, right?"

The pain sitting in the pit of his stomach then had nothing to do with anything except her. He yanked his right hand from his pocket and held it out. "Adam Fortune."

She looked uncertain, then slowly settled her hand into his.

Unlike Dr. Granger's firm, brief clasp, Laurel's touch felt chilled and tentative. And it lingered. "I'm Lisa."

God help him. He was not strong enough for this.

Don't miss
The Texan's Baby Bombshell *by Allison Leigh,*
available June 2020 wherever
Harlequin Special Edition books and ebooks are sold.

Harlequin.com

HSEEXP0520

Get 4 FREE REWARDS!

We'll send you 2 FREE Books plus 2 FREE Mystery Gifts.

Harlequin Special Edition books relate to finding comfort and strength in the support of loved ones and enjoying the journey no matter what life throws your way.

FREE Value Over $20

YES! Please send me 2 FREE Harlequin Special Edition novels and my 2 FREE gifts (gifts are worth about $10 retail). After receiving them, if I don't wish to receive any more books, I can return the shipping statement marked "cancel." If I don't cancel, I will receive 6 brand-new novels every month and be billed just $4.99 per book in the U.S. or $5.74 per book in Canada. That's a savings of at least 12% off the cover price! It's quite a bargain! Shipping and handling is just 50¢ per book in the U.S. and $1.25 per book in Canada.* I understand that accepting the 2 free books and gifts places me under no obligation to buy anything. I can always return a shipment and cancel at any time. The free books and gifts are mine to keep no matter what I decide.

235/335 HDN GNMP

Name (please print)

Address   Apt. #

City   State/Province   Zip/Postal Code

Mail to the **Reader Service:**
IN U.S.A.: P.O. Box 1341, Buffalo, NY 14240-8531
IN CANADA: P.O. Box 603, Fort Erie, Ontario L2A 5X3

Want to try 2 free books from another series? Call 1-800-873-8635 or visit www.ReaderService.com.

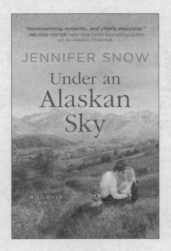

4865

Love Harlequin romance?

DISCOVER.

Be the first to find out about promotions,
news and exclusive content!

f Facebook.com/HarlequinBooks

Twitter.com/HarlequinBooks

Instagram.com/HarlequinBooks

Pinterest.com/HarlequinBooks

ReaderService.com

EXPLORE.

Sign up for the Harlequin e-newsletter and
download a free book from any series at
TryHarlequin.com

CONNECT.

Join our Harlequin community to
share your thoughts and connect
with other romance readers!
Facebook.com/groups/HarlequinConnection

HARLEQUIN

HSOCIAL2020